Also from
Nichole R. Bennett
and Indigo Sea Press

Sleeping Bear

www.secondwindpublishing.com

Ghost Mountain

By

Nichole R. Bennett

Stiletto Books
Published by Indigo Sea Press
Winston-Salem

Stiletto Books
Indigo Sea Press
302 Ricks Drive
Winston-Salem, NC 27103

Copyright © 2009 by Nichole R. Bennett

First Stiletto Books edition published January, 2016
Stiletto Books, Moon Sailor and all production design are trademarks of Indigo Sea Press, used under license.

For information regarding bulk purchases of this book, digital purchase and special discounts, please contact the publisher at
www.secondwindpublishing.com

Cover design by Stacy Castanedo

Manufactured in the United States of America

ISBN 978-1-63066-360-5

To my husband, without whose love, support,
and encouragement this novel
would never have been written.

Prologue

"Move."

The gun was small, loaded, and pointed straight at him. It gleamed in the moonlight. With his hands duct taped behind him and another strip of the silver tape over his mouth, Scott Curtis knew he was going to die.

Unfortunately, he wasn't sure why.

The two walked up to the giant monolith. Scott had never seen Devils Tower this close. Nor at night.

For a moment, Scott was in awe of the landmark. It seemed to jut out of the ground with an unnatural force. The sliver of moonlight didn't do much to illuminate the Tower and the shadow it cast over the paved path reminded Scott of a phrase his grandfather often used to describe the night sky—"blacker than black."

Distracted as he was, Scott managed to trip over a stray rock which had found its way to the otherwise smoothly paved path, causing him to fall to his knees.

"Get up."

Scott continued to lead the way, not that he had much choice since the gun was pushing into the small of his back. His arms, wrists and shoulders ached. The tape itched. His mouth was alternately filled with saliva he couldn't choke down and dry with fear over what was happening. His mind raced, wondering what was in the backpack casually slung over the killer's shoulder.

They reached an area where the path was surrounded by fallen rocks and Scott wondered if he could use one to cause a diversion or to bash his tormentor in the head and get the hell out of there. With his hands bound behind him, though, he wasn't hopeful.

"Stop. Sit."

The killer—and there was no doubt in Scott's mind of how this escapade would end—finished the last swallow of the soda brought along from the car. The sight reminded Scott of how thirsty he was. He expected the killer to throw the bottle to the ground. What was a little littering if you were getting ready to commit murder? Instead, the bottle was placed next to the black boots covering his captor's small feet.

His executioner had taken great pains not to be noticed, dressing in clothing that was dark, yet didn't automatically seem nefarious.

Clothing that was loose enough to be worn to the gym, yet dark enough to hide blood splatter. Clothing that was easily purchased at any number of discount stores and could be easily disposed of without causing too much suspicion one way or another.

Scott wondered if these were items normally found in his captor's closet, or if they'd been purchased specifically for this occasion.

"Wanna smoke?" The killer chuckled. "No, I guess you don't. Well, maybe you do, but I ain't taking the tape off anyway, so it doesn't matter."

The smell of smoke filled the air as the assassin lit a cigarette, still keeping the gun pointed at Scott. He'd had more than an hour to formulate an escape plan, but one kept eluding him. He wanted to put up a fight, but the pistol discouraged that more than he cared to admit.

"I thought about trying this another way. Really I did. I hope you know it's nothing personal, Scott."

Scott glared in the direction of the voice. The executioner's dark clothing—jeans, boots, and especially the oversized sweatshirt with the hood up and the baseball cap to hid the platinum hair Scott knew to be covering the head—made it difficult to make out facial features, but the glowing embers of the cigarette occasionally illuminated his tormentor.

"I just can't have you ruining things." His captor fieldstripped the cigarette and stomped out the remaining embers. The killer tossed the used butt into the backpack, then pulled out a roll of duct tape and ripped off a strip.

Scott briefly wondered what this piece was for and would have asked had his mouth not already had some of the shiny tape over it. How long had he been held captive? The events of the past few hours seemed a bit murky as he tried to remember them all.

Picking up the used soda bottle, the killer began to tape the spout to the barrel of the pistol. Never did the gun leave Scott, though, again dissuading him from an escape attempt. He wished he was brave enough to make a run for it, and was saddened, although not surprised, by the realization he wasn't.

After what seemed like an eternity, the task was completed. The killer pointed the gun squarely at Scott's chest.

"*Es tut mir leid.* I'm sorry. Please understand. I can't let you expose him."

Scott winced in anticipation as the murderer squeezed the trigger.

1

"Cerri, have you seen my other shoe?"

"Mom, Zach is bothering us!"

"Am not!"

"Are to!"

I felt a headache coming on.

The movers honked as they pulled into the driveway, bringing with them most of our worldly possessions.

"I so hate moving," I announced to no one in particular as I knelt on the living room floor, rolling up the sleeping bags we'd used the night before. I also hated sleeping in a house with no furniture. I'd done enough of both growing up as a military brat.

Tonight this house would feel like a home.

"Yep, but you so love an adventure, don't you, Cerri?" Matt, my loving—but somewhat annoying—husband mocked as he came up behind me. "Seriously, though, do you know where my other shoe is?"

"How would I know? You've lived here longer than I have."

We had moved to Cogan Ridge in western South Dakota because Matt had landed his dream job as an Associate Professor of Geology at South Dakota's School of Mines and Technology. My man loved rocks. Matt had already been living and working in the area for two months while I took care of everything back home. It worked well at the time, but I was glad to have my family together again.

"Don't you have to go to school?" I asked, finding his shoe beneath a pile of blankets.

"You're right. I'm outta here. I have a department meeting this morning." His lips brushed mine, leaving the taste of peanut butter on my lips. "Enjoy putting all the stuff away."

I shot him a dirty look as I tossed a pillow at him.

He laughed and tossed the pillow back before letting the movers in as he headed out the door.

The four burly men dressed in dark blue pants and shirts with the moving company's logo across the back added to the already chaotic whirl of activity. How they managed to avoid the gang I affectionately called my "three monsters," who were chasing each other from room to room, is beyond me. I couldn't really blame the kids, they had been cooped up in the car all day yesterday. Secretly,

I was glad we'd only moved four hundred miles away and not farther. Being trapped in a car with a seven-year-old boy and five-year-old identical twin girls for eight hours straight was not my idea of a good time. I couldn't imagine ever making the trip again.

I tried to snag my towheads, sending each one to get dressed before they resumed their game of "catch me if you can."

As I directed the movers to put boxes here and there I admired the job Matt had done picking out our house, a four-bedroom Craftsman-style bungalow in a new subdivision just outside the city limits of Rapid City. Remembering all the moves I'd been through in my life, I knew I'd have to thoroughly search the house for spots the kids could hide. That thought brought an onslaught of memories, and I remembered how my Irish mother used to sprinkle each doorway and windowsill with salt every time we moved. She claimed it kept out evil spirits. I learned later that ants also don't cross a salt line and we never did have ants in our homes.

I spotted a large black ant on the kitchen countertop and knew I'd have to find the table salt and do some sprinkling of my own. Evil spirits, if they even existed, couldn't be trapped in our home. We would be the first family to live there.

As movers brought in another load of boxes, my son, Zach, chose his room. The girls found one they wanted to share. After assigning Matt and I the master bedroom—complete with walk-in closet and a full bathroom—the final room would be mine. Mine to use however I wanted. I hadn't totally decided if it would be a sewing room, an office, or both. Right this minute, I was looking forward to having my very own kid-free zone.

Sobs from the other room broke into my thoughts and I hurried to find the source.

"Mommy! Zach stole my bear!" Mackenzie wailed, putting me on high alert. This was the kid who never cried, which is why her big brother often picked on her, while leaving Madison alone. Madison wore her heart on her sleeve and therefore wasn't the challenge Mackenzie represented.

"Zach! Give the bear back to Kenzie. Now." It only took one warning to make that happen.

Madison was sitting on the floor, holding on to her own bear tightly, and making a face at Zach. "Told you you'd get in trouble." Her superior tone was unmistakable.

"Maddie. Not the time, honey." Once again I was surprised at how alike Mackenzie and Madison looked, but how different the two girls could act. Their personalities may have been total opposites, but there wasn't anything they wouldn't do for each other.

Zach took a few steps toward Madison before being distracted by the movers. The box in their arms didn't need a label; the picture of the television was enough of a clue.

Hooking up the twenty-seven-inch set was easy. The DVD player, on the other hand, took a little more time. As I was fiddling with wires, one station ran their noon news program. The top story had something to do with a body found in Wyoming and I vaguely wondered how close we were to the state line. Or if there were so few news stories locally that they had to find things in other nearby, yet sparsely populated, states to fill the airwaves. Geography had never been my best subject. I was much better at English and math.

Finally, the telltale blue screen of the DVD player came on, cutting off the reporter. All three children simultaneously accosted me with their selection of movies to be played immediately.

The day wasn't getting any easier.

The sound of knuckles lightly rapping on the wall interrupted my thoughts.

"Excuse me, Cerr . . . um . . . Kerr . . . um, Mrs. Baker? I need your signature." The supervisor, a big, burly guy with more hair than sasquatch covering his arms and peeking out from under the collar of his shirt, handed me a clipboard with our cargo manifest for me to sign.

As I took the form from him, I prepared myself for his inevitable next question.

"Unusual name ya got there. How's it pronounced?"

I was right. "It's Cerridwen, but most people shorten it and pronounce it like 'Carrie.'"

My tone didn't encourage further comments. I couldn't blame the guy for being curious, but I'd spent my entire life explaining my unusual first name and the novelty of it had worn off long ago. Cerri rolled off the tongue much easier than Cerridwen, a pre-Christian Celtic goddess most people had never even heard of. Goddess of femininity and the moon, the original Cerridwen was said to have prophetic powers and divine knowledge. My mother celebrated her Celtic heritage by naming her oldest child after one of her favorite legends. I often wondered why Mother couldn't have been fascinated with the Wild West's Annie Oakley or, if she had to be so proud to be Irish, why not Brigid, the country's patron saint. Then maybe I would have had a "normal" first name.

As the movers left, I was again regretting the decision to uproot our lives. The kids had run me ragged, and I didn't get as much unpacked as I had hoped. I wanted to have a home-cooked meal ready for Matt when he got home, but it didn't look promising. I wasn't even sure which box the dishes were in. My mother always made moving look so easy.

The pizza delivery boy showed up minutes before Matt.

After dinner, I got the kids calmed down and ready for bed using my special bath salts, the scent of which reminded me of the baths my mother prepared when I was growing up. Mother made sure we knew she didn't use those salts simply for their pleasing aroma.

I shook the memory away. I didn't want to carry on *that* legacy.

My mother came from a long line of what she called "wise women." She claimed to embrace the power of the Earth, summoning spirits from each of the four directions. She would gaze into water and allegedly see the future. She would even use herbs and crystals to solve everything from colds to heartache. I remember when I had my heart broken as a teenager; Mother's cure wasn't a pint of chocolate ice cream. Instead, she placed a mixture of herbs and flowers in a pouch, chanted over it and then told me to carry it everywhere for a week. Looking back, I guess I should be grateful Mother didn't encourage me to eat my feelings, but I'm not sure the pouch did much either.

During the full moon, she used to chant over all the coins she could get her hands on: pennies, nickels, dimes, even our piggy banks weren't safe. Mother claimed the chant attracted more coins— and thus more money—to our household the rest of the month. While we never lacked for anything, I still believed it was because Dad had an extremely stable occupation. Army generals don't usually lack for much.

Mother claimed she could communicate with spirits, as well. To me, that seemed more like listening to her inner voice than anything else.

Heck, for all I knew, Mother still did all those things and then some. It wasn't a part of her life I wanted to hear about, so I didn't call Mother as often as she would have liked. Parlor tricks and lucky guesses don't make people normal. As an adult, I'd found normalcy to be exactly what I needed in my life.

Maybe it was the act of moving, but right now I was overly sentimental and sort of missed Mother, Dad, and even my younger sister Wendy.

Wendy was my exact opposite. Where I was a fair-skinned and redhead like Mother, Wendy had the darker complexion of our father's mixed heritage. Part English, part German, part Danish, part

Native American, Dad claimed to be pure mutt.

Looks weren't the only difference between my sister and I. She not only embraced the mumbo-jumbo of the spirit world, she actually studied the stuff. Or maybe the correct term was *practiced* the stuff.

I never understood her fascination with all that hocus-pocus and superstition. I've never seen much difference between thinking that a broken mirror will lead to seven years of bad luck, or drinking a rosemary-spearmint tea to improve your mental focus, or saying a chant to help find a lost item. All were superstitions from less enlightened times.

If you look hard enough, you'll find whatever was lost. A little relaxation, with or without any type of tea, will help you focus, and there's no such thing as luck. Some things are good, and some are bad, that's just life. This may be an overly simplistic view, but it's worked well for me.

In some cases, though, knowing the properties of a particular herb can be helpful. The bath salts I preferred, for example, were very relaxing. The combination of sea salts and jasmine, lavender, sandalwood, and chamomile essential oils smelled divine and, since I made them myself, were so much cheaper than buying the pre-made concoctions from the specialty store at the mall.

Another tradition I decided to keep was to have our home surrounded by flowers. Mother had flowers in our home year round and I grew up loving the smell and look of them. There were Violets in the spring said to encourage love, Sunflowers in the summer for prosperity, the protection of Solomon's Seals in the fall. Often our lawn looked like a gardening catalog exploded all over it, but the beauty and scent says *home* to me.

I was in my early teens when I learned that all flowers have meaning, not just red roses on Valentine's Day. That's not why I liked flowers, but I found the idea interesting. So if I kept a bit of Queen Anne's Lace—which was said to keep a home safe—and a touch of Feverfew—for health and protection—near the front steps, I did it because of the beauty of the plants. Putting a few Lotus pods in a dried flower arrangement had nothing to do with the fact that they supposedly mean good luck and blessings. Keeping dried lavender around the house was more for its fantastic scent than because I believed it offered some kind of protection from bad luck.

Unfortunately, sometimes Mother really does know best.

2

Matt and I got the kids to bed with only one request for a glass of water—a record since Zach almost always asked for at least two. I took that as a sign that they were as tired as I was. Heading back to the living room, I plopped on the couch with a force I would have scolded the kids for using.

"Rough day, Cerri?" Matt sat next to me with much less oomph. He grabbed the remote from the coffee table and turned on the TV. A local station was running a commercial for the upcoming late news.

"A body was found early this morning at Devils Tower National Park. Details at ten." The perky young anchorwoman's look of concern couldn't have been phonier. At this moment, I didn't care about a body at Devils Tower. I was more concerned with tomorrow's weather forecast.

"You have no idea how rough," I said. "Have I ever mentioned how much I hate moving?" I laid my head into the crook of his shoulder.

"But you're so good at it," Matt whispered.

I could feel, rather than hear, his chuckle. While I enjoyed the adventure of living in a new place, the hassle of moving was something I could do without. Thanks to Dad's military career, we were at a new base every two years. Sure, I lived everywhere from Texas to Belgium and saw more things before I left for college than most people see in their lifetimes, but the idea of packing up and moving all the time filled me with dread.

"You know what?" I asked.

"What?" Matt kissed the top of my head.

"I never want to see another moving box in my life," I said seriously. "Promise me we'll be here for a long time. Promise. Not just for me, but for the kids, too." My career as a freelance writer and photographer allowed me to visit a variety of new places, especially when I was working for travel magazines, but I needed a permanent place to call home.

I must have started to doze, because the next thing I knew, Matt was telling me to go to bed.

I don't actually remember going to the bedroom, but I must have. I realized I must be dreaming because I suddenly found myself in the now immaculate kitchen, dressed and pouring myself a cup of coffee from the full pot on the counter. I always drink at least one cup of coffee before my shower and, in this instance, I was already wearing more than my pjs. Besides, all the boxes seemed to have been unpacked.

In reality, I only had a vague idea which box contained the coffee maker.

As I looked around the kitchen, I saw He Who Waits sitting at the table as if waiting for me.

When I was younger I looked on He Who Waits as my invisible friend. He was always there when I wanted to play or needed to talk. As I aged I began to think of the grandfatherly Native American medicine man as a manifestation of my imagination. He Who Waits didn't speak English as his first language. I knew this the same way a honeybee knows which flowers to visit. English was the language I usually heard him speak, though. A few words—like *cuwitku*, which meant "daughter"—I somehow heard in his native tongue. I'm not sure how I knew what those words meant. I just did.

No matter how old I got, though, every time I imagined what my conscience might look like, I saw He Who Waits in my mind's eye. He was my own Jiminy Cricket. As a little girl, I had tried discussing this part of my vivid imagination with my mother once, only to be reminded that she had named me after the all-knowing Goddess Cerridwen for a reason. Overall, that didn't help.

"*Cuwitku*, it has been many moons."

"Hey, buddy, where've you been? Like the new house?" I honestly didn't know what to say to an imaginary friend anymore. That talent usually leaves people when they stop believing in such things. I searched my brain trying to remember the last time I'd even thought about He Who Waits. It had been years.

He Who Waits scanned the room. "Yes, *Cuwitku*, this is a good home. And close to the sacred places of the people."

I took a seat across the table from him. Conversation with him seemed the normal thing to do, but what is normal in dreamland? His long, salt-and-pepper hair was tied in a ponytail. As I studied his face, it was hard to tell if the many wrinkles came from time or environment. It struck me that He Who Waits could have been dried like a raisin and gotten similar results. Even in my dream, I could smell the leather of his pants and shirt. I fought the urge to reach over and touch the soft, tan-colored suede.

The non-dreaming part of my brain complimented my imagination on its attention to detail.

"I am not imagination, Cerridwen. I am your *Tuwe Ya*."

Just as it didn't bother me how I knew *Tuwe Ya* meant "guide," I wasn't overly concerned with He Who Waits knowing my thoughts.

"No, you're a dream. Big difference," I mumbled, as I watched myself write *TUWE YA* on a napkin left on the table from dinner. I wondered briefly where the pen had come from but didn't dwell on the thought.

He Who Waits continued as if I hadn't spoken. "You are among the People now. *Paha Sapa* is a spiritual area. *Paha Sapa* is important to the People."

I wrote *PAHA SAPA* on the napkin, wondering—not for the first time in my life—what tribe He Who Waits was from. I assumed I learned about his tribe in elementary school, though I never remembered doing so. Or else my father, who was some small part Native American, must have told me these things when I was a little girl.

He Who Waits didn't seem to notice my lack of attention. "*Mato Tipila*, the Bear's Lodge, is sacred within *Paha Sapa*."

"Okay. So this Bear's Lodge place is sacred. I don't understand what that has to do with me. I mean, I'm sure it's a nice place and all, but why tell me it's sacred?"

"You must understand Bear's Lodge. You must find the answer and restore *Mato Tipila* to its sacred state. Someone has desecrated it. The spirits will not rest until justice is served. It is your *ozuye* to see justice done."

As if it had a mind of its own, my hand scribbled *OZUYE* on the napkin with the other words I didn't understand.

I replied, "Yeah. Sure. Whatever."

"Remember my words, *Cuwitku*," He Who Waits said. "They will come to pass."

The medicine man stood, nodded at me and started to walk away. His apparition seemed to dissipate a little with each step. When he was almost completely transparent, He Who Waits turned around to face me again. He looked directly at me while clapping his hands once.

In the blink of an eye, my immaculate, organized kitchen had returned to its earlier state. Moving boxes and all.

And He Who Waits was gone.

3

The next morning the family was back to struggling to get routines set. Matt had already enrolled the kids in school—Zach in second grade and the twins in kindergarten—and planned to take them. Obviously, they'd missed yesterday, but school had only started the previous week. I wanted to be in South Dakota over the summer, but Matt and I decided to wait until our old house sold before the kids and I joined him.

As I was clearing muffin wrappers and juice boxes that made up our breakfast, I noticed a napkin on the floor. I picked it up and saw the notes I'd written the night before.

"Damn," I mumbled as I read the words I barely remembered writing: *PAHA SAPA*, BEAR'S LODGE, *MATO TIPILA*, *TUWE YA*, and *OZUYE*. The words stared at me as if daring me to find meaning in the foreign phrases. I started to get that sick feeling in the pit of my stomach. The same one students get the moment they realize they've forgotten to study for a major test.

Instead of wasting time trying to decipher the meanings, I did what any intelligent woman would do in a situation she couldn't immediately wrap her mind around—I shoved the napkin in my pocket and tried to forget about it.

There were too many boxes left to unpack.

No matter how hard I tried, though, I couldn't completely forget the napkin I'd shoved away. When I least expected it, my thoughts returned to the scrap of tissue and the conversation with He Who Waits. By lunchtime, I knew I would get no rest until I discovered the meanings of the words I'd written.

Matt had made sure to have the Internet hooked up when the phone and satellite were connected, so I turned on my laptop to see if I could figure out a way to translate the words.

I logged on and within minutes my sister, Wendy, sent me an instant message.

How's the Great White North? she typed.

Wendy, who had been a drama major in college, had perfected the habit of exaggerating. I replied:

I wouldn't know. I'm only one state north. Not a big difference between Nebraska and South Dakota. It's not as if I've been gone for years, you know. I just saw you the other day.

How's Matt's new job?
She also had a habit of changing the subject without notice.
It's not really a new job you know. He's been working here for two months.

I was trying to search the phrase *Paha Sapa* while we chatted. When it came up on the screen, I saw the familiar shape of Devils Tower. The site claimed that *Paha Sapa* was the Lakota name for the Black Hills, which stretched from western South Dakota into Wyoming. Reading a little further translated *Mato Tipila* as the Lakota phrase for Devils Tower.

The picture on the screen didn't seem to have much in common with the ominous Devils Tower I remembered from movies.

The *ding* of another instant message brought me back to the conversation with Wendy.
Yeah. I know. So what's with the body?

Her words reminded me of the television report I vaguely remembered from last night.

I hated it when Wendy brought up items in my life she shouldn't have a clue about. Usually, I could convince myself she found out what was going on with me from our parents and then used the information to catch me off guard. Other times I convinced myself she was just a good guesser. Either way, though, messing with my head was one of my sister's favorite hobbies.
What are you talking about?

Don't play dumb. I saw it on CNN.

I used to swear she spent more time with electronic media then I did. Even though I have a degree in mass communications, it's Wendy who has her television set to the twenty-four-hour news channels. The woman is a news junky. It wouldn't have surprised me if most of the internet sites she visited were newspapers and television stations. I'd rather play solitaire on my computer when I wasn't actively working on an article.

Wendy and I spent the next few minutes discussing what she knew, which was actually a lot more than I did since I hadn't been paying attention. According to Wendy, National Park Service officials found a man's body at the base of Devils Tower. Some reports even claimed the man had been shot multiple times, but that wasn't confirmed. I wanted to ask her why she even cared, but knew there wouldn't be an answer to that. For Wendy, the fact it was on the news made it an interesting topic of conversation.

He Who Waits's words came back to me. *"Someone has*

desecrated Bear's Lodge." Well, at least I knew what he meant now.

BTW, Wendy typed, *I pulled the Two of Cups for you this morning.*

That was odd. Wendy almost never used Tarot cards. She preferred using runes, but it didn't stop her from trying her hand with a deck once in awhile. It was one more area where Wendy and I were different. I liked the cards, even though Matt often teased that Mother had ingrained them into me. To me, the cards and the amazing, symbolic artwork that went with them pointed to options and caused me to think about things in a different light. However, like the daily horoscope, you could always read something more into what the cards represented.

Strangely, the Two of Cups meant honoring one's gifts, but Wendy shouldn't know anything about my previous night's adventure.

Hey, Wen, I typed, *I need to go. Still have boxes to unpack.*

Okay. Be careful, Cerri. I have a bad feeling. Promise you'll be careful!

Then she signed off without waiting for my reply. Another of Wendy's bad habits was how she ended conversations. They were over when she decided, and she usually had to have the last word. Even when we were kids, she'd stick her fingers in her ears to signal the end of a conversation.

But to type the words *be careful* and then sign off was incredibly annoying. Leave it to the drama major to try and give me more to worry about. Wendy must not think moving caused enough stress in my life.

By the time the school bus pulled to its stop, I was ready for the distraction of my children. Maddie and Kenzie talked non-stop until dinner, then Zach took over.

"And then this one boy, he let me sit by him at lunch. And then there was this other boy, and he was really funny. And there was this one girl. She's yucky. I had to sit by her and she always raised her hand for everything. I think she likes to pretend she's really smart, but I don't think she really is."

Zach was talking so fast I couldn't be sure he was actually breathing.

Matt grinned over his glass of iced tea as he listened to his son ramble. "You know, Zach, you might end up liking those smart girls one day." Matt winked at me as he spoke. "Look at your mom. She's pretty smart, and we both like her."

Zach gave his dad a look that said he wasn't sure how smart his dad was. "She's a mom. She has to be smart," he said matter-of-factly.

Kenzie and Maddie then had to throw in their opinions about the smarter sex, both thinking that boys were dumb, especially brothers.

"But daddies are prob'ly pretty smart," Kenzie said with a grin.

The chatter continued until bedtime, with each child proving how smart he or she was.

Once the house had quieted down and "one more" drink of water had been doled out, Matt and I were able to talk while doing the kitchen chores. Even though we had a dishwasher, I washed and Matt dried. Having Matt's undivided attention every night while we did the dinner dishes was our special time when we got some of our best talking done. Since only one interesting thing had happened to me during the day, I relayed everything I'd learned from my sister about the body.

"Yeah, I heard that on the radio," Matt replied. "From what I understand, they aren't sure what the guy was doing there to start with."

"That's what Wendy said. Isn't Devils Tower just a big rock, though?"

"Cerri, it's a beautiful rock. Seriously. It's majestic." Matt's eyes widened as he spoke about the country's first National Monument. "Did you know that almost every Native American tribe has a myth about it? It's phenomenal."

I looked at my usually calm husband as if he'd lost his mind. "Last time I checked, many cultures had similar myths. How many different cultures have stories about a world-wide flood?"

"You're right. But it's a beautiful rock, babe." Matt put the last of the dishes away and hung the towel to dry on the side of the sink. He leaned over and gave me a kiss. "I'm beat. I'm going to hit the sack early. Do you mind?"

Of course, I didn't. I needed the time to find answers to the mysteries of the previous night.

I hit the Internet hard, searching for anything I could find on Devils Tower and the news story circulating the airwaves. On the five o'clock news there hadn't been much new information about the body, only that a man had been found at the base of the tower. According to what I could find between different television and newspaper websites, the body had been hidden just off a hiking trail on the north side of the rock. Of course, no one was releasing the victim's name or how he had been killed. I certainly wasn't going to go hunting for those answers.

With no new information on the death, I decided to search again for the words I'd heard from He Who Waits. I found most of them on a Lakota translation site, and deduced that He Who Waits was my *Tuwe Ya*, or guide of some kind, and he had information about my life's mission, or *ozuye*.

More for me to think about.

4

He Who Waits was sitting on the living room floor. I really hadn't expected to see him again and wondered why my imagination seemed to be working overtime lately. I hadn't dreamt of this guy for at least fifteen years and now it had been twice in once week.

"*Cuwitku*, you have learned very little about my people." It wasn't a question. He Who Waits spoke quietly, as if trying not to wake anyone. I had to step closer to hear what he had to say.

"Why are we whispering?"

The elderly Native American regarded me with a degree of sadness in his deep brown eyes. "You do not yet understand, Cerridwen. I am not a *wowihanmna*. I am not your imagination. I am your *tuwe ya*. I come to you at night, but not in sleep."

"So I'm not sleeping? You're trying to tell me that I'm wide awake?"

That was it. It was official. I was nuts.

He Who Waits stood, silently moving from sitting on the floor to standing in one fluid motion. It surprised me the way the older man could be so quick yet so quiet.

"You still do not understand. I have been with you always. Do you remember a time when I was not available?" His expression reminded me of a disappointed grandfather trying to explain something to a stubborn child. Just looking at him made me feel a bit guilty, as if I had done something I shouldn't have.

Walking toward the couch, I sighed. "You're right, I don't understand. I'm talking to a dream. Granted, you're a great dream and all, but still a dream. An imaginary friend I created to help with the stress of moving every few years as a kid. Therefore, I must be stressed out now, too." I sat down on the soft cushions, curling my long legs beneath me. "Or maybe I'm going crazy since I'm talking to myself."

He Who Waits rubbed a leathered hand across his forehead as if trying to fight off a headache. Intrigued, I watched as he seemed to search for a way to explain.

"No one can go through this life alone. There is help for all. Some are blessed with the ability to see. Others to hear. You have both." He Who Waits looked at me, as if trying to find the next words. "Many do not believe. They try in vain to understand that which is not understandable. They choose to ignore the gifts they have been given."

He continued on, reminding me of times when I was younger. The words he'd given me then had foretold of one event or another, anything from an upcoming move to answers on a pop quiz in school. Over the years I'd convinced myself that I could tell when my family would move by paying attention to how long we had been stationed at each base. But, knowing test answers was either the result of paying attention in class or studying harder than I realized.

Either way, those weren't really psychic talents. Those were the results of being observant.

"Okay, so you're saying that you've given me information to 'predict' the future, right?"

The Shaman nodded once.

"Why? What was the point? If I believe you—which I pretty much don't—the Lakota have a belief that everything happens for a reason, right? So what was the reason for me predicting the future? So I would know when my dad got stationed somewhere else? So what? Who cares? Nothing I could do about that stuff." I could feel my throat tighten and hear my voice start to rise. Pretty soon I'd be ready for a cozy room with padded walls.

He Who Waits didn't miss a beat. "You are not *wacinhununi, Cuwitku*. There is a purpose to everything."

Pretty sure the shaman had just pronounced me sane, I leaned my head back against the couch and closed my eyes. This was getting to be too much for me to take in. Even my hallucination thought I was sane. Did that make me officially crazy?

I felt a depression on the seat beside me and vaguely wondered if imagination could cause an indentation in the couch. I didn't really want to open my eyes in order to find out but, logically, I didn't think so. Then again, the image of the shaman seemed so real, why wouldn't my hallucination extend to an indent on the couch?

The deep bass voice and cultured English of He Who Waits interrupted my thoughts. "You were granted the sacred gift of seeing and hearing the spirit world, *Cuwitku*. It has been my responsibility to watch out for you since the day you were born. All have a place in the Circle and your place is to find justice for those who do not receive it."

I opened my eyes and looked at the man or the spirit or the vision or whatever he was. "You're here to help me find justice. For who exactly? What kind of justice? Only for big things? Or everyday small injustices, too, like someone stealing a parking space? Why didn't you bother me before?"

As if he could sense a shift in my perception, a smile of relief passed over He Who Waits's face before he answered me in the same slow, patient voice I'd become accustomed to hearing. "What is different is that you are now in a more sacred place. It is now more difficult for you to ignore what you have. Your mission has not changed. The option of ignoring your gifts has."

It took a moment for his words to sink in. Deep in my soul I knew he was right, but I sure didn't want to admit it. Why couldn't I just be normal?

He Who Waits laughed, deep and loud and throaty, and I thought for sure he would wake the kids—had he not been a dream, of course. He shook his head and smiled. "You are now starting to understand. I see it in your eyes. I hear it in your thoughts."

"Fine. I get it. So what am I supposed to do?" I continued as the Indian—I mean, Native American I'd read somewhere that the term "Native American" was more politically correct—opened his mouth to speak. "There's injustice everywhere. Am I supposed to be some kind of super hero, out to fight the bad guys of the world?"

"For now, only one. You must learn who desecrated Bear's Lodge. You are to help the police bring justice. To . . . how did you put it? Catch the bad guy?"

"Great," I mumbled. "I'm named after an Irish Goddess and have a Lakota Sioux Spirit Guide bossing me around. Great."

There was another throaty laugh, lightening the mood in the room. "You are blessed with spirits from both sides of your family tree, *Cuwitku*. The magic within you runs deep."

Shaking my head, I brushed the hair out of my face. I might as well try one more time to get out of this mess. "Look, you may not realize this, but the police don't really appreciate the help of civilians. They think they can do a better job fighting crime than most people, and frankly, I tend to agree with them."

He Who Waits nodded. "Yes. They do an adequate job. But it will be difficult for them to find all the information. It will be faster if you help. Justice will be swifter."

"Any idea how I'm supposed to do this?"

"That is for you to discover. I will tell you what should be known at this time and you will find a way to impart the knowledge. The *wosnapi* is named Scott Curtis and resided in Rapid City. He did not go willingly to Bear's Lodge. The young man was shot two times by someone who knew him. I cannot give you any more information right now. You must tell those who can help."

While He Who Waits spoke, I walked over to the bench near the front door where I had left my purse. Rummaging inside the hobo-style bag, I found an old grocery receipt and a pen. I wrote down the information as fast as I could and stuck the paper in the pocket of my flannel pajama bottoms. I looked up to argue one final time against the mission He Who Waits seemed to think I had.

The shaman had already gone.

5

I stared at the spot where He Who Waits had just been, seriously questioning my sanity. If I were sane, I apparently now knew more about the body found in Wyoming than I should.

It suddenly occurred to me that the crazy never realized they were totally nuts. If I were crazy, though, I would believe I'd been talking to a spirit of some kind.

"Damn! I'm turning into my mother." There would be no going back to bed now. I'd pay dearly for the lack of sleep later, though, since sun wasn't even up yet.

In a daze, I walked back down the hall to the spare room where my laptop was. I had it booting up as I carried it back to the living room. I wasn't going to think about ghosts or spirits or any other type of hocus-pocus. Obviously my imagination was running overtime as it was.

When I checked my e-mail, there was a short note from my sister Wendy, saying that she was still following the news report about the dead body found at Devils Tower and asking what the news here was saying.

"Can't I get away from this?" I spoke just loud enough to hear my own voice. As I rubbed my temples, I sincerely hoped Wendy was going to let it drop. I knew better.

Actually I couldn't remember the last thing Wendy had let go. Except maybe her ex-husband, but even he was more booted out, rather than calmly "let go."

Rather than answering her, I checked my other e-mails, wondering if I would have any assignments from one of the various magazines or newspapers I usually did freelance writing for.

Freelance writing has been an interesting profession. I've been able to satisfy my taste for travel and meet some really interesting people while having a place to call home. In addition, I've done things like fly in a World War II-era P-51 Mustang for a story about an air show; meet a famous country singer when he performed a concert; and interview a Presidential candidate on the campaign trail. Granted, not all my stories had been exciting, but I also don't ever remember complaining of a boring day at the office.

Plus, I've been able to stay home with the kids, which is even better than seeing my by-line appear in a national magazine.

At least, I think it is.

Okay, so I'm probably a 1950s housewife born a bit too late. Sue me.

An e-mail from a children's wildlife magazine editor I occasionally worked for popped up. Sarah Martin and I had graduated college together and kept in touch. While I decided to form my career around my family, Sarah had taken the opposite track eventually becoming the youngest managing editor the national magazine had ever seen. The arrangement proved beneficial to us both. She congratulated me on our move and asked me if I'd be interested in writing an article on Devils Tower. Sarah's e-mail stated:

We're covering a number of national monuments in the next year. Since Devils Tower was the country's first, it's only logical that it be the first one we cover.

I couldn't believe what I was seeing. "This is ridiculous! I'm sick of Devils Tower!" My voice was a touch louder than I had meant it to be, but the coincidences piling up were really getting to be a bit much. And I had grown up being told there was no such thing as coincidence.

Now, I wasn't sure what I believed.

Matt stumbled out of the bedroom, rubbing his dark brown eyes. "What? What's ridiculous? Is there any coffee?"

After setting the laptop down, I followed him into the kitchen and started a pot of coffee. Neither Matt nor I could be considered "morning people," and we both need to be jump-started in order to face the day. Matt could at least have pleasant conversations until the coffee finished brewing. I, on the other hand, was lucky to grunt appropriately before my second cup.

I looked up at the clock on the kitchen wall. 5:30 a.m. I didn't know how long I'd actually been awake since my conversation with He Who Waits, but I certainly didn't feel tired. Confused and frustrated? Yes. Tired? Not really.

"I'm sick of Devils Tower."

"That's a new one. Most people around here get sick of Mount Rushmore first. And how can you be sick of either one after two days? We haven't even done the tourist stuff." Matt ran his hand through his dark hair as he yawned. The smell of java began filling the room, and I could almost see Matt start to awaken as his senses responded to the aroma.

Grabbing two coffee cups, I prepared to pour us each some of the dark, steaming liquid: Matt's straight black, mine with cream and

21

sugar. The heat from the mug warmed my hands before I even realized I'd been cold. "I just keep hearing about the monument, that's all."

Matt cocked his eyebrow at me as he took a sip. "Yeah, right." There was no mistaking the tone of his voice. Maybe it was the way I couldn't look at him as I answered, or maybe it was the fact that I could answer him at all this early in the day. Either way, he knew I was bluffing.

I sat at the table while Matt scrutinized me with his scientist's eye. I felt like a microscopic specimen waiting for him to dissect. "You done staring?"

Snatching the peanut butter toast he'd made while I'd poured coffee, Matt sat down across from me. "Nope. You have something on your mind. I can tell." He didn't pause as I opened my mouth to interrupt him. "Don't start, Cerri. I can tell when something's bothering you. And the move ain't it."

"You know I hate it when you do that." Honestly, though, I hated it when anyone assumed they knew what was going on in my mind. Either I continued to find myself surrounded by people who thought they were mind readers, or else I must be very predictable.

Matt took a bite of his toast. "Yep. I know you too well." The peanut butter stuck to the roof of his mouth as he spoke. It was times like these when I knew exactly where Zach got some of his more annoying habits. "So what's really going on?"

I told Matt about the writing offer from Sarah and mentioned that I'd found more information about Devils Tower. I did not bring up anything about spirits or justice or dreams involving the monument, let alone my visit from He Who Waits. There wasn't much I kept from Matt and I disliked omitting information now, but that part of the story sounded ridiculous even to my own ears. If I couldn't believe I'd been talking to my own imaginary friend, how could I expect Matt to believe it?

In the condensed form I presented, the frustrations of earlier sounded silly. "I guess I'll be making a trip to Devils Tower in the next couple of days. How far is it, anyway?"

"Plan to spend the whole day there, Cerri. It's probably an hour and a half or two hours to get over there. After you get your photos and interviews and whatever else you need, it will be an all-day event." Matt shoved the last of his toast into his mouth, brushed the stray crumbs off the table and onto his plate, then stood up to put his dishes in the sink. "What's the angle of the story?"

We spent the next few minutes discussing the points I had

already considered, as well as the information the editor had sent my way. By the time Matt shared his ideas for the story, he had to hit the shower and I needed to get the kids up and ready for school.

The routine worked well for our family. Since I was lucky enough to stay home most days, I got the kids up and dressed while Matt was getting ready. He then tried to arrange his class schedule each semester so he could take the kids to the bus stop on school days. I made sure to be home for them at the end of the day.

Chalk it up to one of the benefits of being self-employed.

Zach, Madison and Mackenzie were all out of bed, dressed, and had eaten breakfast as Matt was ready to head out the door. Throwing a monkey wrench in the routine, Matt asked, "Hey, kids, how about I take you all to school today? Since Mom's got to finish unpacking, you can ride the bus home."

His suggestion was met with a round of enthusiastic "Yeahs." I was grateful that we'd taken the time last night to show the three scholars where to catch the morning bus. Matt had registered them weeks earlier. They would know where to get off so I wouldn't have to worry about them ending up lost, which was one of my greatest fears when it came to the kids.

When the crew was all out of the house, I headed for the bathroom to prepare for another day surrounded by moving boxes. The steamy, hot shower not only felt good on my sore muscles but also kept my mind from wandering. I was sick of the spirit world. What I really wanted was the physical labor of unpacking the house; something guaranteed to tire my body.

I stepped out of the shower, dried off, and slipped into a pair of jeans and an old T-shirt. There was no need for makeup or nice clothes if my day was to be spent between rearranging furniture, deciding where to place those little trinkets that make a house look truly lived in, and doing preliminary research for a magazine article. I knew I'd be writing the story, no matter how badly I wanted to stay clear of Devils Tower. There was no reason not to do it.

Sweat ran down my back from my non-stop exertion and I'd long since found a handkerchief to tie around my head, keeping my curly, reddish locks from escaping into my face. Thankfully, though, the kitchen was almost finished, with appliances set up and most of the dishes placed in the cupboards. The only task left in that room was to put away the rest of the pans and a box of canned food I'd brought with us. That was the good news.

Unfortunately during the day, I'd broken a nail while putting together a computer desk and snagged a hole in my sock when I tripped over a small, wooden trinket box my mother had given me when I was a teenager.

I lifted the box labeled PANS and heard the familiar clinking of glass. Inside, along with a plethora of metallic cookware, was the turkey platter Matt and I received as a wedding gift. The glass platter was now in four very large pieces and many more much smaller ones.

"Damn movers! Something always breaks." My frustration level was high. I knew I needed a break but was too stubborn to take one.

"Things can be replaced, *Cuwitku*. Broken lives can not." The stilted English of He Who Waits came from behind me.

Maybe I could ignore him by collecting the pieces of the broken platter.

"You must help fix lives," he said.

"Yeah. So you've said." I turned around to face the intruder, placing my hands on my hips in frustration. "Look, I'm a little busy right now. I don't really have time to have any kind of nervous breakdown."

The ancient Lakota shaman slowly shook his head. "You do not yet believe. You are *tahu suta*, Cerridwen. It makes you fair and righteous, but difficult to work with."

It didn't take a rocket scientist to figure out He Who Waits had just commented on my stubbornness.

"We are running out of time," he added sadly.

I grabbed the box again and headed to the cupboard I'd reserved for the cookware. "Look, I'm busy, all right. I'm obviously having some sort of delusion, probably brought on by the stress of moving. Let me finish unpacking and then I'll have time for a breakdown." I thought if I just continued to put things away, the entire experience would soon be forgotten. In an effort to act normal, I knelt on the floor to put the pots and pans away.

A crash behind me caused me to whip around. He Who Waits had ripped the silverware drawer out and all the eating utensils were strewn about the floor. The clanking and banging of the dinnerware as it hit the linoleum floor was loud and unexpected.

"What the . . .?" My previous plan of pretending to be sane was temporarily abandoned as I stared at the mess I'd have to clean up. "There was no need for that!"

"You must listen. You must do what you are called to do." He Who Waits stood calmly next to the counter, despite the havoc he'd just caused. At least *he* didn't seem to mind the extra work I was now going to have to do.

"So if I don't do what you tell me to you're going to tear apart my house? That's a bit harsh, don't you think? Even for a spirit." There was really no denying it. He Who Waits was not a figment of my imagination—unless, of course, imagination could move things. I'd never heard of that before. I made a mental note to call Wendy and ask her how to get rid of him.

"I will not leave." The expression on the shaman's face proved I wasn't the only stubborn one here. "We made a contract before you came to this Earth, *Cuwitku*. I will honor my word and expect you to as well."

As I recognized the truth in his words, a wave of resignation swept over me. There would be no getting rid of this spirit. If I'd learned anything from Mother, it was that spirits could, and would, do what they darn well pleased. I groaned as I realized the implications of that thought. I was becoming more like my mother every day.

"There's no getting out of this."

He Who Waits chose to ignore my mutterings. "You must call the authorities. They will not succeed without you. It is your destiny."

It was pointless to argue. I grabbed a phone book and began flipping through the pages, wondering whom I should contact. Maybe, once this is finished, he'll go away, I thought. Somehow, though, I knew that was wishful thinking on my part.

Years of watching my mother and sister deal with spirits gave me a basic understanding of the boundaries, but I didn't like the rules nearly as much when I was the one dealing with the otherworld. And somehow it didn't seem fair that I had to clean up the mess on the floor some spirit made, while the two people who knew more about this kind of thing weren't being bothered with messages from beyond.

While I was looking up the number for the police station, I remembered part of a news report I'd read online the night before. I thought it had mentioned an anonymous tip line for the crime.

I booted up the laptop and found the tip line phone number. Surely, an anonymous clue would be investigated. Plus, I could get this spirit off my case and get back to my own life.

Since I was so nervous, it took three tries to dial the correct number. The call finally connected, and I was able to spew out the information I knew into an answering machine without ever talking to a real person.

"Um, yeah, I, uh, wanted to tell you that the body at Devils

Tower is Scott Curtis from Rapid City. He was shot twice. At close range. And by someone he knew. You, um, should look at people he knew."

The entire message lasted only five or ten seconds because I was talking so fast, but it felt like it had taken much longer.

Thank goodness for technology.

After I hung up the phone, I turned around, ready to face He Who Waits and let him know that I had made the call. The authorities were contacted. And He Who Waits was free to leave. For good.

He wasn't there, though.

Unfortunately, the scattered silverware was.

6

I watched the news reports that night, hoping for information about Scott's murder. It surprised me that I had quit thinking of him as "the body" and began thinking of him as an actual person. That I knew his name before it was released to the media made the tragedy that much more real—and creepier. The entire situation disturbed me.

I was glad when Friday came around. The house was mostly unpacked and I was ready to relax.

As if I thought it would work out that way.

Minutes after Matt and the kids had left for the day, the phone rang. I recognized the number immediately. Mother.

As difficult as I found her, she was still my mother and I did love her. But I would never understand her.

"Hi, Ma." I answered the phone, using the affectionate Irish term for "Mom."

Her soft Irish lilt responded with, "Cerridwen, my lass, I hate it when you do that. Can't you just answer the phone with a hello and pretend to be surprised that it's me?"

I chuckled. "Nope. Caller ID allows me to annoy you that way."

Mother was never one to dwell on technological advances for long. "Well, how's the new house?"

"It's nice," I replied. I told her about the house and a little about the area since I didn't think Dad's Army career had ever brought my parents to the Black Hills of South Dakota.

After a few more minutes of small talk, Mother dropped her bombshell of a question. "So what are you doing with the murder up there?"

"What?" I felt my heart flop to the pit of my stomach. Of all the things I would expect to come out of my mother's mouth, that wasn't one of them.

I could almost envision my mother rolling her bright, green eyes as she moved the hair off her shoulder. Mother's hair had been always been curly and carrot-like in color and cascaded down to the middle of her back. Recently, the invading grey hairs gave it more of a strawberry-blonde hue.

"Now, Cerridwen, my dear, you know what I'm talking about." Mother's strained voice carried that same tone which expressed frustration with small children. "The body found at Devils Tower. That's not too far away from you, is it?"

"No, Ma, it isn't. And I'm sure the police have everything under control. How's everything there?" Experience had taught me that attempting to change the subject was pointless, but I had to try.

"Well, have you been paying attention? I get the feeling that you're going to be involved. In fact, I know you will, my dear. And you haven't lived there long enough to know the poor man. You didn't know him, did you?" Mother continued as if I hadn't spoken.

"No, Mother, I didn't know this guy." I sat at the kitchen table, picked up a pen and started doodling on a sale ad that came in the morning's mail. "I don't know him. I doubt I would have ever met him. And I certainly am not going to be meeting him now, am I?"

"Cerridwen, behave. You have a mission, you know. I thought long and hard about your name. You have much of the Goddess in you."

Here it was again, how I was named after a goddess with prophetic powers and divine knowledge. That meant I had a responsibility to the Universe and I needed to stop fighting my destiny. I'd heard the lecture so many times I could probably recite it with her. Even now it was all I could do not to roll my eyes as Mother spoke.

Once again, I thought Mother should have named my sister after the Goddess. She appreciated the nonsense that went with the name much more than I ever could. But it didn't work that way. My sister got the normal name and inherited the interest in this gibberish. I got stuck with the name and wanted nothing to do with the rest of the nonsense.

Mother—or the Universe or fate or whatever—obviously had a sick sense of humor.

By the time Mother finally stopped ranting, I was more than ready to end the conversation.

"Okay, Mother. I have to go now."

"One more thing, dear. You'll be involved with this murder . . . with solving it, I mean. Pay attention to what isn't said."

"What isn't said?"

"Yes, Cerridwen, what *isn't* said. You still study that, don't you?" Mother was clearly referring to classes I had taken in college on reading body language. I'd always been fascinated with communication, including the non-verbal messages people don't realize they project. "Also, look for a large man. He'll help you find justice for the victim. Watch for him, Cerridwen. It's important. He's important. Must go now. Kisses to all."

And with a click, she was gone. Conversations with my mother were often like that: straight to her point, and over when she said so. Just one more way Mother and Wendy were alike.

I barely had enough time to hang up the phone myself when the doorbell rang.

Running through the house, I managed to fling the door open before my visitor had the chance to ring the bell a second time. On the other side of the door stood a mountain. The man, dressed in a dark suit and what I thought of as a power tie, stood well over six feet tall and reminded me of a rectangle. His shoulders, hips and feet seemed to be made of straight lines. If he wasn't a professional football player or Marine, he should have been.

I silently berated myself for not checking the peephole. It was something I'd forgotten only a handful of times in my life.

"Can I help you?" I wasn't sure what help I could give, since the man obviously had the wrong house and I didn't know any of the neighbors. I didn't even know where anything was to give directions. As the man's size actually began to sink in, I offered a silent prayer that he was merely going to ask for directions and wasn't some crazed psychopath who decided to stop at our house on his mass murdering spree.

It occurred to me that I needed to quit watching so many Alfred Hitchcock movies.

"Are you Cerridwen Lynn Baker? Married to Matthew James Baker, an instructor at the South Dakota School of Mines and Technology?" The man's voice was deep, quick and rough. He kept his large hands at his side; cupped in a manner I recognized military members using while standing at attention. I'd seen Dad do it numerous times.

"Who are you?" I must have looked pretty shocked, but there was no way I was going to give this stranger any information about me, even if he seemed to already have the information. I'd never been that stupid.

"Special Agent Joseph Oliver, FBI. May I come in?" His cold eyes flashed around me, looking into the house as if he were taking in his surroundings. I didn't think much escaped his attention.

"Not without a badge." I'd never had the FBI or any other law enforcement agency show up at my door before, but I was pretty sure I should ask for something like that.

I never saw him reach for it, but he produced a thin, black wallet with his picture, an ID, and a gold badge on the opposite side of the billfold before I had finished asking the question. I didn't know what I was looking at, but it looked legit to me. I invited him in.

"Thank you." He stepped past me and into the house. An air of power surrounded him. Intimidating wasn't a strong enough word for this man.

"I'm not sure what I can tell you, sir . . . Officer . . . Agent Oliver . . ." I paused. What I was supposed to call the man standing before me? "We just moved here," I said closing the door behind him and hoping he wasn't a serial killer, posing as someone from the FBI.

He followed me to the kitchen where I offered him a glass of water or tea.

"You are Cerridwen Lynn Baker, correct." It wasn't a question. I could tell that he knew precisely who I was, but I had no idea how he knew.

What do you say to an FBI agent in your home? Is there a correct protocol for that?

"Is there something I can help you with? I don't understand why you're here." I hoped that sounded more like a statement than a question. It occurred to me that maybe this was part of a background check for some new assignment of Dad's, although I'd never met one of the "background check guys"—as my sister and I called them when we were growing up—so rude and downright scary.

The mountain-sized man continued as if I hadn't spoken at all. "How well did you know Scott Curtis?"

"Who?" I mumbled the word before I could even comprehend what he had asked. His rudeness made the biggest impression on me. This man must have gotten his manners out of a Cracker Jack box.

"Scott Curtis. He was found at the base of Devils Tower. I'd like to know how you knew him." The agent's steel grey eyes stared at me with such intensity I had to look away.

My throat went dry and there was a hole in the pit of my stomach. I wanted to vomit. Even without looking in a mirror, I was sure I had lost all color in my face. Stammering, I replied, "I didn't."

I could see the man's jaw muscles clenching as he stared me down.

Agent Oliver took a deep breath. "You called the tip line yesterday. You gave the name of the victim and knew he was from Rapid City. In addition, you knew other aspects of the crime that had not been released to the public. Now, I'll ask you again. How well did you know Scott Curtis?"

It was my turn to take a deep breath, hoping it would steady my nerves. It didn't. Instead a new wave of nausea hit me like a brick wall. I was pretty sure an answer like "Well, this spirit told me Scott's name and how he was shot. Why don't you grab an Ouija board and ask the spirit these questions?" would cause me more trouble than I was already in. I wondered if I looked as sick as I felt. A corpse probably had more color than I did, although that thought didn't help the sinking feeling in the pit of my stomach.

"I thought those tip lines were anonymous."

"You aren't answering my question."

"Well, this will sound a little crazy . . ." I shoved my hands in my pockets and started to gnaw my lower lip, two nervous habits I'd had since childhood.

"Try me," he said in a not-very-convincing voice.

I didn't want to sound like a fool, so I bent the truth a little. I explained to Agent Oliver that I had gotten the information from a dream and even if it wasn't totally reliable, I thought someone in authority should know what I had seen. All the while, I was desperately hoping I didn't sound like an escaped mental patient.

The agent's cold stare never wavered. "So you're telling me that all of this information came to you in a dream? You never met Scott Curtis and have no idea who killed him, yet you claim to certain details of the crime?"

"Crazy, huh? It sounds crazy to me, too. I was only trying to help." I gave a feeble smile.

"Do things like this happen to you often, Mrs. Baker?"

"I'm not sure what you mean. I certainly don't get visits from the FBI every day."

"Do things like this happen to you often? Do you get visions in dreams? Do you see ghosts? Are you claiming to be psychic?" Agent Oliver's voice had gone from no-nonsense interrogator to warden of the loony bin.

Obviously my explanation didn't sound sane.

"No!" I answered quickly and with too much emphasis. "No. I'm not psychic. This is the first time I've ever had an experience like this, and I hope to make it my last. Look, the information I had, I probably overheard somewhere. And I do have an overactive imagination. I'm sure it's nothing. You guys are the experts, right? You probably already know who did it and everything." I could tell that I was talking quickly and repeating myself, another of my nervous habits.

Maybe that would convince him I wasn't the kind of person who calls tip lines for every little thing, trying to earn my own fifteen minutes of fame through someone else's tragedy.

Tragedy. What if he thought I was the murderer? Didn't criminal masterminds always try to insert themselves in the investigation in order to find out what the police know? I was pretty sure that's what they did on television.

I imagined a file being started on me in Washington. Did the FBI still keep files? Or was that another myth of the Bureau, like so many that involved J. Edgar Hoover? More importantly, did it matter?

Another wave of nausea hit me full force and by now my stomach had sunk to my toes. I couldn't imagine ever feeling normal again.

The look on Agent Oliver's face told me he didn't quite believe me. "And a dream is how you know this information?"

I nodded. "Yes. And that's all I know. Honest."

"You will let me know if you think of anything else that might be helpful, won't you." It wasn't a question.

Nodding again, I felt like a reprimanded child.

"Here's my card. I'll be in touch as well." With that the agent handed me his business card.

I followed him through the house to the front door. I held it open for him as he left.

It wasn't until I shut the door behind him that I was able to breathe again and even then it was another hour before my pulse returned to normal. I cursed my mother, my sister and my spirit guide as I started the mindless task of organizing the linen closet.

7

Since the arrival of Agent Oliver on my doorstep, I had become jumpy. The previous feeling of calm was gone and tight nerves, sore muscles, and a stress headache had taken its place.

My tension was lousy for me, but good for the house. Even as a child, when I would get upset, I would clean. I have scrubbed bathtubs and toilets, rearranged cupboards, even found the time to sort socks if I was upset enough. There was something about the act of putting the things around me in order that seemed to help me order my thoughts as well.

Since we had just moved, though, I opted to hang pictures and rearrange knick-knacks. Again.

If Matt noticed my increased stress level, he didn't ask about it. I wasn't sure how to bring up the subject, either. "Hey, Matt, you'll never guess who showed up on the front step. It was the FBI!" didn't sound like the dinner conversation I wanted to have. Especially since Matt didn't know I'd called the tip line in the first place.

Instead of worrying about the FBI or mysterious spirits or dead bodies, I tried to establish a routine and carry on as if everything were fine. After unpacking the last of the boxes, I decided to immerse myself in work. Anything to keep my mind occupied on the living.

First thing on the agenda was to inform the editor of the children's magazine that I'd like to write the story on Devils Tower. Well, maybe I wouldn't really *like* to do the story, but I knew I would anyway.

After a few e-mails and a phone call to magazine editor Sarah Martin, I knew the angle she had in mind. The magazine was planning to cover some of the natural landmarks of the United States. With a target reading audience of ages eight through twelve, the article didn't have to be too in-depth, but they did it need to be interesting and include a lot of photographs.

My first step was to check out what was available online. There was a National Park Service site that listed information about the various national monuments, and Devils Tower was no exception. The site gave me most of the background information I would need for the story, plus a phone number to contact a park ranger for an interview. Another phone call set up an appointment for Monday morning.

With all that done, I decided to check my personal e-mail account and basically kill some time before the bus brought Zach and the twins home from school. I had started to relax until I heard the familiar *ping*, announcing an instant message.

Wendy.

Mom says you're stuck.

The deep orange of her text was simultaneously warm and accusing. I sighed.

Sure she does. But don't worry, I got everything unpacked just fine.

I had barely hit the return key to post my message when Wendy replied.

Not what I'm talking about. And you know it.

Great. How am I going to get out of this conversation?

Wendy, like our mother, could be a single-minded pit bull.

Then what are you talking about?

Maybe playing dumb would keep Wendy from bringing up anything about spirits or ghosts.

What do you know about the dead guy? Heard anything more from the other side?

Yep, she was a pit bull.

Look, Wen, this isn't my thing. Can we talk about something else?

I suppose. Won't change anything, though.

When I didn't respond, she continued.

Even if you don't want to help, you've been chosen. Nothing you can do about it. Can't outrun fate, you know.

Rolling my eyes, I typed back:

Fate has nothing to do with it. There's no reason for me to get involved. I didn't know the guy and I have no stake in his life or death other than to be sorry he lost his life. Very human reaction.

At times like this I appreciated the fact Wendy didn't like to talk on the phone much. As a nine-one-one operator, she spent her professional life answering calls and chose other forms of communication when off duty. I was grateful she couldn't hear my frustration, or the sarcasm, seeping through my voice.

It was almost a full minute before Wendy replied. I'd begun to hope she'd given up or lost her internet connection. But then more of her words appeared on my monitor.

Fate has everything to do with it.

34

More like my overactive imagination and increased stress from moving has me daydreaming. Big deal.

Nothing happens without a reason, you know. And you and I both know this isn't your imagination.

All of my brilliant arguments and command of the English language failed me. I typed the first thing that came to mind:

Whatever.

Great argument, sis. You know I'm right, btw.

I wanted to scream at her. I wanted to tell her that she wasn't right. It wouldn't do any good though since she was much too far away for any conversation like that. Come to think of it, a face-to-face conversation wouldn't have solved much, either. I should have learned pit bulls don't listen well.

While I was trying to decide what—if anything—to type back to Wendy, my sister continued her one-sided argument.

I know you're going to help. That's your nature. You can't stand it when someone is treated unfairly.

She'd hit a bull's eye. Except in this case that particular character trait was in direct opposition to my desire to mind my own business.

You can't help it, Cerridwen. Comes with the name.

She added a smiley face to the end, as if that would make her statement easier for me to swallow.

Wendy knew how much I hated being named after a goddess. We'd had the conversation many times over the years.

Another *ping* interrupted my thoughts.

It don't get more unfair than murder.

The harsh reality of Wendy's words hit me like a ton of bricks.

Look, Wen . . . I started to type.

Her message came through faster than mine.

I know. You have to go. I'll light a blue candle for you, okay?

According to tradition, the color blue helps people think clearly so lighting that candle would invoke the sprits to assist me in clearing my mind. At least my sister was trying to help. In her own way.

Wendy was right. Glancing at the computer's clock, I saw that the bus would be here any minute.

Sure. I guess that would be okay.

My reply sounded lame to me, but I knew it would make Wendy happy.

Hugs to all. Catch ya later.

With that, Wendy signed off, once again leaving me with more questions than answers.

I didn't have time to worry about my so-called fate, since I could hear the bus in the distance. I had about ten minutes from the time I first heard the bus until it reached our street.

One of the advantages to Cogan Ridge was the number of young families in the area. All three of my kids had found playmates on the block and two young teen girls lived just across the street. Laughter filled the streets shortly after the bus starting dropping off children.

Our house was on a corner lot with a nice-sized yard. As long as the weather was cooperating, I decided to use the time to spruce up outside. I had wanted to mark off a section of the yard for an herb garden, as well as decide where to plant some flowers I hoped would bloom come spring. There was nothing more relaxing than fresh chamomile tea, or the smell of lavender from your own garden and I couldn't imagine a yard without tulips blooming in the spring, even if they were the original "love" flowers.

It seemed like only seconds later when I heard the deep groan of the bus's hydraulic breaks.

"Bye, Madison! Bye, Mackenzie! Bye, Zach!" I heard two voices call as my kids ran, laughing and screaming into the yard.

I noticed that Kenzie was flushed, probably panting more from excitement than from the run across the yard. "Mommy, can Meghan and Bobbi come over to play?" She asked the question as one long word with no opportunity for a breath during it.

"Who are Meghan and Bobbi?"

Maddie answered. "Mommy, they're so nice! They live over there and sit by us on the bus." Based on the direction she was pointing, I deduced that Meghan and Bobbi were the teenagers who lived across the street.

"Not today, kiddo. But maybe they would like to baby-sit Friday."

A chorus of resounding "Yeah!" met the idea. I stood, brushed what little dirt I'd accumulated from the future garden off my jeans, and headed across the street with my three kids following close behind.

One of the teens answered the door within seconds after I rang the bell.

"Hi, Bobbi!" My three kids simultaneously yelled a greeting to the petite dishwater blonde who answered the door.

"Hi, kids. Is this your mom?"

I extended my hand. "I'm Cerri Baker. I was wondering if you and your sister could baby-sit Friday night."

After a quick check with Meghan and the girls' mother, it was decided that the pair would be over around five o'clock so Matt and I could go to dinner and a movie—a treat we hadn't indulged in for a while.

"Great. I'll see you both then," I said before the kids and I headed home.

By the time Matt got home from work, the kids and I were putting dinner on the table and the smell of marinara sauce and garlic bread filled the house. Spaghetti with meatballs has always been one of my personal comfort foods and I needed the comfort.

"Yum! Something smells good." Matt followed the statement with a kiss on my cheek.

Maybe my life was getting back to normal after all.

But for some reason I didn't think I could get that lucky.

8

This was definitely a dream. I didn't need to pretend.

I seemed to be hovering in an apartment I'd never seen before, a few inches above the ground. There were two entities beside me. Since I recognized He Who Waits, I didn't think in terms of *people*, but I didn't know who the woman next to him was. The three of us reminded me of a scene from Dickens's *A Christmas Carol*.

I took a moment to study the woman. In some ways she reminded me of Mother: her hair was the same reddish hue, her eyes the same deep green. Although she was probably a few inches shorter than me, she seemed taller, more powerful, and more commanding. She wore old-fashioned garments. Not the ancient Native American clothing of He Who Waits, but even older. Flowing robes encircled her. The most notable thing, though, was the air of nobility exuding from her.

As she looked in my direction, I automatically lowered my eyes. Something about her made me hope I didn't disappoint her.

To avoid her gaze, I decided to take in my surroundings. Based on the size of the rooms, I deduced we were inside an apartment. The decor was obviously male—dark and sparse—with no telltale sign of a woman's touch bringing color to the rooms. The living room, where I stood, had been straightened in anticipation of company. The pile of old newspapers and the line of miss-matched shoes indicated the room hadn't been cleaned in a while—at least not in a way most women would have considered it being done. Without ever seeing the kitchen I knew there were dishes piled in the sink. I assumed the bedroom and bathroom would be bachelor-pad messy, as well.

He Who Waits nodded in my direction, and I wondered again why he was here.

"To give you knowledge," came his answer.

"And her?"

"She is your namesake. She guides you as well."

So the woman beside He Who Waits was apparently my subconscious's idea of what a Celtic goddess should look like. Great. Maybe I'd lost my marbles, after all.

"Why doesn't she just show up, like you do? You know, anywhere she feels like." I was still upset at having to clean up the pile of silverware He Who Waits had dumped on my kitchen floor. I probably would have kept going, but the look I got from the other Cerridwen stopped me short.

"It is easier for her when your mind is clear. Much of what we learn resides in our subconscious before we fully understand it."

I took his words as the admonishment they were meant to be and vowed to change the subject. Before I could ask where we were, though, a knock on the apartment door stopped any further conversation. From the other room, a young man hurried toward the door. He was tall, well-built, tan and blond. I couldn't see his eyes, but I knew they would be green with flecks of gold around the edges.

How did I know this? I turned toward the two specters, hoping to get an answer to the question. A nod from the goddess stopped me. I no longer needed to ask. I knew. For one split second, I possessed the same divine knowledge she did.

This was Scott Curtis's apartment. And he was still alive. Gotta love dreams.

"What are you doing here?" Scott was obviously not expecting whoever was at the door. I couldn't see who it was, but a whiff of perfume indicated it was a woman. I vaguely wondered why the divine knowledge thing wasn't working this time but, since this had to be a dream, I didn't dwell on it.

"I needed to see you." The woman's voice held no real accent. In fact, other than being female, there was nothing distinctive about it. Her tone sounded forced, though. Like she didn't *want* to talk.

"Yeah, well, this really isn't a good time." Scott looked nervous; his gaze darting past his unexpected visitor as if he hoped no one would see them together. "I'm expecting someone. Can't this wait until tomorrow?"

"No, Scotty, I'm afraid it can't," came the cool reply. "We have a matter that really needs to be discussed."

"I can't think of anything I have to discuss with you. And nothing that can't wait until morning." Scott made a move to shut the door.

"Wait!" she yelled as she held her hand up to stop Scott from shutting the door. Her tone was more urgent, and I thought I detected a faint accent. "I came all this way to talk to you. And . . . and my car's acting up. Can't you at least hear me out?"

Scott sighed. "Look, I'm expecting someone. I don't really have time right now. Tomorrow. I promise."

I tried to see the woman's face, but she kept moving her head, so I never got a good look at her. Her hair was covered by a black hoodie. I got the impression she was trying to disguise herself without actually wearing a disguise. Nothing about her was familiar. Not that I expected her to be.

"Can you at least look at my car? I think it's a fuse or something, but I'm not sure."

Scott closed his eyes and rubbed his hand across his forehead. I could almost see his inner struggle between wanting to get rid of this mystery woman and an underlying desire to help. It seemed to be the classic "stand-up-and-disappoint-someone" versus "be-a-doormat-but-not-let-anyone-down" struggle. Finally, Scott looked back at her. "Fine. Let's go."

Scott stepped into the hall, shutting the door behind him. I wanted to follow and tried to open the door Scott had just closed.

He Who Waits stopped me. "Wait, *Cuwitku*. You are not meant to follow. The events you are seeing have already happened. You can not stop them."

"Then why show me?"

I expected the Lakota shaman to answer. Instead, I heard the Irish brogue of the goddess. "Because you do not need those details. Not at this time, anyway."

I wanted to argue with her. I started to argue with her. One look from the goddess shut me up immediately. I tried to remind myself this was a dream, but I didn't feel as confident in the assessment as I had moments ago.

Our surroundings had changed. In the blink of an eye, we were no longer in the apartment; we were in a parking lot. I could see Scott's visitor pointing to a dark blue or black KIA Sportage. She got in and tried to start it, but nothing happened.

"Pop the hood." Scott walked to the front of the compact SUV and looked at the engine. Since I didn't know anything about cars, I couldn't tell what he was messing with.

"It won't work will it?" I asked the spirits on either side of me.

"It will work in the way it is destined to," said He Who Waits.

The goddess's voice boomed. "Enough! Watch, daughter."

I was right, the car still didn't start.

"Hey, do you know where the fuse box is in this thing?" Scott asked, as he closed the KIA's hood.

"I think it's over here, under the glove box." The mystery woman headed toward the passenger side of the car and opened the door.

Scott started to kneel down when she grabbed his head and smashed it into the car's door jam. Scott's body went slack. I gasped. There was a sigh from He Who Waits and I thought I heard a "tsk" escape Goddess Cerridwen's lips.

Any delusions I'd had about dreaming were gone. I was watching the events leading up to Scott's kidnapping and eventual murder and there was nothing I could do to stop it. I tried to scream at the woman, but no sound escaped my lips. I looked at the Goddess Cerridwen and at He Who Waits. Neither seemed to have any way to stop what we all knew was going to happen. Or else they chose not to.

In the "dream" or whatever it was, I closed my eyes and rubbed my hands against my forehead in a vain attempt to erase the images I'd seen. When I opened my eyes again, I wasn't in the parking lot anymore. The entire ghostly contingent was in another parking lot surrounded by a wooded area. I could tell time had past because it was darker, but we had to be farther from the city because there were so many stars sprinkling the night sky. I was in awe of the sight until I heard a car door slam.

About fifty feet ahead, I saw a woman climbing out of the KIA. She walked around to the passenger side of the vehicle and opened the door. Scott got out. His wrists were bound together, but from this distance I couldn't tell what restrained them. A shock of silver over his mouth told me duct tape kept him from calling out. His eyes quickly swept from side to side, no doubt looking for some means of escape.

I followed Scott's gaze until it rested on a flash of blue-black metal in the woman's hand. Guns had never held much fascination for me, so I couldn't identify this one. The handgun wasn't very big, but even I knew it would still be enough for the deadly shots that were to come.

The woman looked Scott over, letting her gaze move up and down his tense frame. She reached into the pocket of her hoodie and pulled out a pack of cigarettes. She expertly slid one cancer stick out of the pack and finished extracting it with her mouth. She put the pack back in the jacket and removed a lighter from the front pocket of her jeans. Neither her eyes nor the gun ever left Scott's body.

"Wanna drag?" she asked.

Scott glared at her, still unable to talk since she hadn't bothered to remove the tape from his mouth. The fear in his eyes had been replaced with contempt. He looked as if he'd rather spit at her.

She laughed, but it wasn't a pleasant sound.

She pointed the gun at Scott and told him to move. The two walked up the concrete path, toward Devils Tower.

This wasn't going to end well, but for some reason the spirits and I weren't following. I didn't know how to move in this other form, so

I literally couldn't follow. There was nothing I could do except feel my frustration build, knowing I wouldn't be able to stop what was coming.

I think the two were gone for fifteen or twenty minutes. I wanted He Who Waits or the goddess to say something, but neither did. They just stood next to me, as if absorbing the atmosphere. The sound of gunshots broke the night's silence and my thoughts. It was too late to save Scott now.

A few minutes later, the woman returned to the SUV and drove off.

Still not being able to move, I could only watch. What was I supposed to do now?

"The woman Cerridwen will find justice for Scott," said He Who Waits.

"Yes. She will," concurred the goddess. "She will see that justice is done. It is her calling."

The next thing I knew, I was lying awake in bed, Matt snoring beside me. As I listened to the comforting noise, I realized that I now knew two more facts: Scott was kidnapped from his apartment. And the police should be looking for a woman.

Now I had to decide what to do with this information.

I didn't like the idea of another chat with Agent Oliver, but I wasn't sure how I could avoid it.

I didn't sleep well the remainder of the night.

I must have dozed off at some point, because I woke up Saturday morning to the sun's blinding rays. The kids celebrated their lack of school by getting up extra-early and watching cartoons in the living room. The majority of the noise coming from the room sounded more like giggles and grunts than real conversations.

I could smell coffee and bacon and knew that Matt was up and busy. Experience told me there would also be eggs and hash browns waiting in the kitchen and that I would eat the large breakfast, despite the fact I wasn't hungry. Memories of last night's dream had come flooding back to me, causing my stomach to go on immediate strike. Kidnapping, murder, and bacon should not be able to co-exist.

Slowly, I made my way to the kitchen and found my predictions accurate. Matt cooked rich, heavy meals and ate like a horse while never gaining weight. I thought about a piece of chocolate and gained two pounds.

"Smells good," I mumbled.

He turned around long enough to give me a kiss on the nose before returning to the pan of sizzling grease. "You like your bacon crispy, right?"

"Yep." One and two word answers were all my tired brain could manage. I poured myself a cup of coffee and added the creamer and sugar I preferred, thinking the caffeine might help.

"You did a great job putting everything away this week. Thanks. I appreciate it."

"Umm, sure." The coffee hadn't kicked in enough for me to speak in long coherent sentences. I snatched a slice of bacon from the plate where Matt had put the cooked pieces, and we discussed what the five of us might do that afternoon. Ideas ranged from taking the kids to one of the free attractions in Rapid City to doing some yard work.

"Frankly, I think we should go somewhere," I said. "Isn't there some kid-oriented park you were telling me about? Story Land? Or something like that?" Visions of the three little ones running around and wearing themselves out made me smile. Midwest winters could get cold and nasty, so this mild September day should be cherished.

"It's called Storybook Island. I think they'd have a great time there," Matt informed me. "Let's go!"

More laughs and giggles filled the next few hours. We got the kids fed and dressed, and then drove into town to find the park Matt had suggested. Armed with my camera, I managed to take some great pictures of Zach, Madison, and Mackenzie climbing on the kid-friendly displays at the park. Fairy tales, television shows and favorite nursery rhymes were all displayed in hard-plaster-like statues for children to enjoy. By the time we left the park hours later, the kids had tired themselves out as I had hoped.

The silence in the back of the van as we drove home was deafening as the kids started to nod off from their busy day.

"So, do you wanna tell me?" Matt's question interrupted the quiet.

"Tell you what?"

"Why the FBI was at our house this week."

For a moment didn't know how to answer. I certainly wasn't going to lie to Matt, but I had hoped he would never learn about the visit. It was obviously too late for that. "The FBI?" I knew I sounded like an idiot, but I was stalling.

"Yep. Found the card in the kitchen the other day. Anything I should know?"

As he drove, I told Matt about the visit, even confessing to my anonymous tip.

"How did you know any of that?"

It was a reasonable question, but it was the one I didn't want to answer. Thankfully, we were almost home. I thought maybe I could avoid answering him by waking up the kids and getting them into the house. By the look on Matt's face, I knew this was only a reprieve and the conversation would be continued later.

I was right. Once the kids had been put to bed, Matt was there, asking again while we did the dinner dishes. "So, how did you know anything about this murder? And don't tell me it was a guess, Cerridwen."

I felt like a small child being scolded. Matt never called me Cerridwen, always Cerri. I couldn't tell if Matt was trying to ensure I gave him a straight answer, of if he thought anything I said would be far-fetched. I almost answered "Gee, Matthew, a ghost told me," but I caught myself in time. I wasn't sure my sarcasm would achieve anything. Instead, I replied, "I just knew. I'm not sure how, but I thought it was important enough to leave a tip."

Matt stopped drying and eyed me suspiciously. "If that's all it was, why didn't you say anything?"

"Because." I washed another glass. "What was I supposed to say? I don't even have any real evidence. Honestly, Matt, I didn't think it was important enough to bother you with." When he didn't respond, I continued, "A little weird, yes. But not that important."

Plus I was sure my scientific-minded husband would have me locked up in the loony bin if I confessed I'd been talking to spirits. I opted for personal feelings of guilt for not telling him everything rather than have Matt think less of me.

I finished washing and leaned against the counter to wait for Matt to finish.

As he dried the last dish, he said, "You could have told me." There was a hint of disappointment in his otherwise macho voice.

"You're right. I should have. I'm sorry." Maybe an apology would be enough to move the conversation on to more pleasant topics.

He was silent for a moment, putting the towel down and turning to face me. "This is one of those things like your mom does, isn't it?"

There. He'd said it. I had tried to avoid that topic, but he brought it up anyway. Matt didn't place any more stock in my mother's beliefs than I did, so it must have been fairly obvious for him to recognize what was happening. Or else I was totally losing it, which actually made more sense.

"Cerri, is this one of those things your mom does?" Matt repeated slowly, as if he wasn't sure whether I didn't hear him or didn't understand what he was asking. His voice was even, but tight, adding to the tension I was already feeling.

I took a deep breath, not wanting to hear my own answer. "Yes," I whispered. "I think it is, no matter how hard I try to ignore it."

Matt didn't say anything but nodded quickly as he closed the gap between us. "You know, Cerri, you can justify almost anything. You're good at that. You are more like your mom and sister than you care to admit." He took a deep breath and looked down into my eyes, wrapping his arms around me in a bear hug. "I think it will all be okay. But you have to tell me what's going on. Deal?"

"Deal." I wasn't sure whether to be relieved Matt was taking this so well or upset that I couldn't hide what I considered to be a huge character flaw on my part.

Either way, I knew my life would change from this moment on.

9

The rest of the weekend passed by uneventfully.

When Monday morning arrived, Matt took the kids to school and I hit the road for the interview with the park officials at Devils Tower.

Matt had been right. It took about two hours to get from the house to the national park. I arrived twenty minutes early for the interview, and was grateful to be able to stretch my legs. Grabbing my camera, I headed toward the majestic rock to shoot some pictures.

I hadn't taken more than a half dozen steps when the feeling hit me. Yes, the scenery was beautiful but a life had been taken here. The sick feeling in the pit of my stomach started to return and I briefly thought about canceling the interview and going home.

I reminded myself that I wasn't really here because of the murder; rather I was assigned to do an article about the monument. No other reason.

At least that's what I told myself.

I took in my surroundings as I tried not to think of the actual events that brought me here. Even with the dry summer the Black Hills had experienced there was enough green foliage at the base of the Tower to make a stark contrast to the brown and gray of the rock. The concrete path may not have made for the most attractive photo, but it provided me with a place to start my own exploring. For a moment I regretted being here so late in the year and wondered how many people had walked the same path during the height of tourist season.

Wandering around the base of the monument, which I remembered reading was a little more than a mile in circumference, I snapped pictures of everything. I learned a long time ago that the more photos I took, the greater the chance I had to get a really awesome shot. In all my years of freelance work, I had never been upset because I took too many photographs.

At the start of the trail, a sign reminded visitors to stay on the path. Another sign, just a few feet farther reminded people once again. I had the feeling these signs would be constant reminders around the Tower. They were the biggest distractions from the beautiful scenery.

A colorful sachet tied to a nearby tree caught my eye. The red cloth had holes in it and was dirty. I couldn't tell if those were the effect of being out in the elements, or if the material had been nothing more than a scrap before it was tied around the small branch. I didn't know what it meant, but I snapped a picture anyway.

I decided to head left, keeping the monument to my right. Still searching for "the perfect shot," I noticed more of the bundles tied to other trees. I made a mental note to ask the ranger about them during our interview.

Rounding the first bend, I stopped. I'd seen this area before. The path, the rocks, the trees were all familiar; although I knew I'd never been here. It took a few more minutes before I realized that this was the area I'd seen in my dream.

This was where Scott had been killed.

"You are correct, Cerridwen." He Who Waits was sitting on a large rock just off the trail. Dressed in his traditional Lakota clothing, he looked as if he belonged in that environment more so than I did with my jeans and tennis shoes.

I almost reminded him that he shouldn't be off the trail before I realized that rule probably didn't apply to the spirit world.

"No one else can see or hear me, *Cuwitku*. I will not leave an imprint on this site." The shaman took a deep breath. "I am here to tell you that you are on the right path. Listen to what the *sun'ka womna* . . . the ranger . . . has to say, but you must listen to your heart as well. You must ask questions the ranger will not want to answer."

I glanced up at the formidable mountain on my right, trying to sort out the questions I had for my companion. When I looked back, He Who Waits was nowhere to be seen. I knew he hadn't really left and would probably show up unannounced when I least expected it, yet again.

Looking at my watch, I decided it was time to head back toward the ranger station for my interview.

Ranger Jean Hill was a tall, sturdy woman with jet-black hair and skin a shade that can only be duplicated by hours in the sun. She had a no-nonsense air about her, but the laugh lines surrounding her pale blue eyes were a testament to her wild side. She wasn't overweight, but I didn't think she would ever be called thin, either. I was positive she could beat me in almost any physical competition.

"Ms. Baker! Welcome to Devils Tower!" Ranger Hill's voice was deep for a woman. That, combined with the faint smell of nicotine, was evidence of a long-standing cigarette addiction. "What can I do for you?"

After she led me into her small office, I explained the type of article I was writing and began to verify the Tower's statistics with Ranger Hill. She went on to tell me about the number of climbers who tried to tackle the eight hundred and sixty-seven-foot hexagonal columns each year.

"And we advocate a voluntary climbing closure each June, which has reduced the number of climbers during that month by eighty percent. We also ask that hikers voluntarily refrain from scrambling within the inside of the Tower Trail Loop."

"Why would you want to reduce the number of climbers and hikers? I mean this was America's first national monument. Wouldn't a climbing and hiking restriction actually dissuade people from visiting?" I remembered reading something about climbers on the mountain, but had only skimmed the details since my article was going to be for younger children.

Ranger Hill laughed, deep and throaty. "You'd think so, wouldn't ya? But it doesn't. We have visitors all year long. And June is important to many Native American tribes. All kinds of ceremonies take place then. In fact, the Lakota people traditionally hold their Sun Dance in June at the base of the Tower. You do know that it's not really from the Native peoples that we get the name 'Devils Tower,' don't you? The phrase is actually from a misunderstanding."

From my preliminary research, I had learned there were many names for the mountain, including Bear's Lodge, but I hadn't found any reference to why the name Devils Tower had stuck.

According to one of the most popular legends, a huge grizzly bear had chased some children to a rock. After the children pleaded with the Great Spirit, the rock grew and the bear tried in vain to capture the children, resulting in the claw marks seen from miles around. The story would make a nice sidebar to my article and the magazine's younger readers would enjoy an adventurous legend dealing with kids their own ages. But nothing there mentioned a devil of any type.

As I relayed my scant knowledge to the ranger, she suggested we walk toward the tower. Though walking and talking at the same time have occasionally caused me problems thanks to a serious lack of coordination, we headed out of the office.

"That's right!" Ranger Hill sounded impressed with what I had learned, no matter how little that might have been. "The children— usually thought of as girls—were raised so high that they were pushed into the heavens and became the seven stars of the Pleiades. As for the name, historians believe one explorer mistranslated the

Lakota name into 'Bad God Tower.' Since European explorers didn't have a 'bad god,' they translated it into 'Devils Tower' and that's the name that stuck."

"Leave it to the white men to not listen," I joked.

Ranger Hill smiled, ignoring my outburst. "The Lakota also received their most sacred object here. The White Buffalo Calf Pipe. It was given to them by White Buffalo Calf Woman, who is an important spiritual being. It's said that the pipe was supposedly kept in a secret cave on the north side of the Tower."

I started to ask where the pipe was now, but the ranger was too intent on continuing her story. She explained that in 1875, General George Custer had sworn by the pipe not to fight the Sioux again. "Legend has it that anyone who swears by the pipe and breaks oaths, comes to destruction," continued Ranger Hill. "And there are similar stories from the Crow, the Cheyenne, the Kiowa, the Shoshone and the Arapaho Tribes. Since this is such an important site for so many tribes, we feel strongly about closing it to climbers for that month."

"Didn't I read that ceremonies are held all the time, not just in June?"

Ranger Hill turned in a circle, scanning the area carefully. "There," she said, pointing to a tree off the path. "See that bit of cloth tied to the tree?"

I did. It looked similar to the ones I'd noticed earlier. This one, though, had a bit of green fabric, in addition to the red.

"That's a prayer bundle. The Native people leave them here all the time. It's as important in their culture as holy water is in the Catholic Church."

I let that information soak in while I took some photos of the ranger with the monument in the background. Ranger Hill graciously continued to answer questions and share her experiences at the Tower. After taking both digital and film pictures, I thought I had everything I needed for a few pages in the children's magazine. One thing continued to bother me, though.

"Can I ask one more question? Off the record."

Ranger Hill's eyes narrowed a bit as she cocked her head to the right. "Go ahead." Her voice had lost some of its joviality, and I detected a serious edge to it.

"You talked about people climbing the Tower, and there was a news report about that body being found here. Do people die here often?" I didn't want to let on exactly how much I knew.

"Since 1937 there have been only five climbing fatalities and they were all while descending the Tower."

"So it's a pretty rare occurrence?"

"Thank God!"

"How would someone get in after the park closed?" I remembered the gate shack I had passed on my way in. Besides a small town, not much was around the shack. I didn't know how many other park entrances there were or if some areas surrounding the monument were more isolated then others.

"That's a good question. There is a fence surrounding the national park land, but it's more of a boundary fence as opposed to something designed to keep people out." The ranger sighed deeply. "We may never know exactly what happened to that poor man."

We returned to the parking lot and ranger station in silence. As I reached my car, I called to the woman heading into the building. "Oh, Ranger Hill! You mentioned that most of the Tower's names had to do with the bear legend. Are there other names?"

A smile once again crept into the ranger's eyes. "Sure! The Lakota also called it 'Ghost Mountain.' No one is exactly sure why, but it probably has to do with their White Buffalo Woman legends."

The drive back to Cogan Ridge seemed to pass quickly, especially once I noticed He Who Waits in my rear view mirror. The shaman had materialized in my backseat.

"Ghost Mountain? Your people called it Ghost Mountain?" I was loud, but thankful that I had the windows up and no one else could hear me.

"Yes, *Cuwitku*. That is one name for Bear's Lodge." The spirit guide's voice sounded confused, as if he didn't see the irony.

"And you don't think it's odd for you to show up, talking about a murdered man whose body was left at *Ghost* Mountain." I stressed the word 'ghost' wondering if he would understand my sarcasm. Maybe one ghost didn't think seeing another at a place called Ghost Mountain was all that unusual.

In the mirror, I saw him nod. "I understand your concern, but one has nothing to do with the other. Bear's Lodge is a sacred site to my people. The *sun'ka womna* explained that. To have it desecrated with death is *si'ca*."

"*Si'ca*? What's that?"

He Who Waits turned thoughtful for a moment, as if searching for the right word. "Evil," he finally said.

I kept driving. The scenery didn't change much, mostly hills, with a few trees and some houses peppered along the interstate. After ten or fifteen miles I spoke again. "What do you want me to do?! I'm not a detective. I'm not a cop. I'm a writer and a mom!" I pounded the steering wheel in frustration, not that it made me feel any better. "I don't even know where to start."

He Who Waits simultaneously vanished from the backseat while materializing in the seat next to me. It must be a testament to how crazy my life was getting when that didn't faze me. At least I didn't almost cause an accident.

"You have already done the first part," began the shaman. "Now you must call again. You know the killer was a woman. The Celtic Goddess showed you that. Take the information and share it with the police."

A sign beside the road welcomed me back to South Dakota. "You know, the police will think I'm crazy. And how am I supposed to give them this information?" My hands gripped the steering wheel a little tighter as I once again struggled with the question of my own sanity. Normal people do not talk to ghosts, I reminded myself. And they surely don't ask ghosts for advice!

"You will find a way," replied the ancient shaman. "It is your *ozuye.*"

The rest of the ride back to Cogan's Ridge was done in silence. By the time I pulled into the subdivision, He Who Waits had disappeared.

Another surprise waited for me in the driveway, though.

Leaning against a non-descript sedan, his arms and ankles crossed, was Special Agent Oliver. He was chewing on a toothpick and wearing an expression somewhere between angry and bored. I wondered if the anger on his face was a permanent feature. A quick glance at the digital clock on the car's radio told me the kids wouldn't be home from school for about forty-five minutes. Hopefully, that would give me enough time to answer his questions and have him leave before the bus pulled up.

"Agent Oliver. How can I help you?" I called as I got out of my vehicle.

"Mrs. Baker, I have a few more questions for you." The FBI agent didn't move, successfully giving the impression that I wasn't worth his time.

"Really, I told you everything I know. I'm not sure what else I can add." I wasn't sure how to tell him the killer was a woman. Sharing that piece of information would secure my spot as either his main suspect or a complete crazy. Neither title I wanted.

Agent Oliver stood and started to follow me. "Well, I have a few things I'd like you to clear up for me."

"Umm . . . sure." Unlocking the door, I let the two of us in the house. I had told Agent Oliver everything I knew about the murder of Scott Curtis—or at least all that I knew when I'd talked to him the first time.

Maybe the Universe was creating a way for me to let authorities know more about what was going on without having to place another phone call. It was obvious from our first encounter that anonymous tip lines weren't really anonymous. The Universe? Yeah, right. I just had rotten luck.

Agent Oliver continued to follow. It occurred to me that he walked much quieter than I expected for someone his size.

As we headed toward the living room, my mind raced to find a way to throw in the new information I had about this murder. Deep down, I knew the FBI had no idea who killed Scott. Self-preservation, however, kept me from blurting anything out.

I barely sat down before the Special Agent started peppering me with questions. His manners hadn't improved since our last meeting.

"Mrs. Baker, you claim that Scott Curtis was shot twice. Where did you hear that?" He remained standing, forcing me to look up at an odd angle to see him.

"I believe, Agent Oliver, that I mentioned it was just a dream. One that felt so real I decided to call the tip line. I only wanted to help." I took a deep breath, trying to steady my nerves. Something about this man made me very nervous. Maybe it was just the fact he was from the FBI. "Would you care to have a seat?"

Ignoring my question, and my obvious discomfort at the angle of my head, he continued. "Yes, you did mention that the details came to you in a dream. What night did you have this 'dream?'" He said the last word as if it was distasteful.

"I really don't remember what night it was."

"You don't remember." It was a definite statement. "And what exactly happened in this dream?"

"I believe I already told you. I had a very vivid dream where I saw Scott be—"

"How did you know the victim's name?"

"I just did. I must have heard it on the news." I knew that wasn't true, since I didn't know the dead man was Scott Curtis until He Who Waits told me. I hoped the lie sounded convincing. Racking my brain, I tried to remember if any stations had mentioned Scott's name. I couldn't think of any.

"On the news, I see." Agent Oliver reached into the breast pocket of his suit jacket and removed the same notebook I'd seen him use during our last encounter. "What station was that?"

"What station?"

"Yes, Mrs. Baker. What news station did you hear the victim's name reported on?"

I rubbed the back of my neck, which was starting to cramp from trying to maintain eye contact with the law enforcement officer, who was still standing too close. "Look, I'm not sure. As I told you last time, we just moved here not too long ago. I'm not even sure what the local channels are yet."

"I'm going to be honest with you, Mrs. Baker, I don't believe you." Agent Oliver's pause was as heavy as he surely intended. "You know more than you're letting on and I intend to find out what else you know. I think you're involved in this and I aim to prove it."

"B-b-but I'm not! I told you! It was a dream! I was only trying to help." Visions of the next fifty years behind bars flashed through my mind as I stumbled to explain myself.

"I want to know *how* you knew this information. The victim's name hasn't been made public. I'll ask you again. How did you know Scott Curtis?"

It was the moment of truth. Should I stick to the dream story or tell Special Agent Joseph "the jerk" Oliver that an ancient Lakota spirit guide told me the name because the Universe is upset that Scott's body was dumped on a holy site? Neither option seemed overly appealing at the moment.

"I'm waiting, Mrs. Baker."

I took a deep breath to steady my nerves. Other than Matt, I'd never told anyone about the "witchy habits" running through my family and I wasn't sure exactly where to start. "Agent Oliver, the name came to me. That happens sometimes in my family. If you don't want to believe it was a dream, that's fine, but I'll tell you I had nothing to do with the poor man's murder."

The agent glared at me, but I decided to keep going. Why had I ever called that hotline in the first place?

"I will also tell you that Scott was killed by a woman. He wasn't expecting her that night, but she showed up at his apartment."

"What else do you know?" Agent Oliver's voice became even terser, an effect I hadn't thought possible.

"I know I had nothing to do with it. I know you're wasting your time here when you could be out finding whoever did this." I was ready for the interview to be over. Out of the corner of my eye, I saw He Who Waits manifest. Nothing good could come of his appearance right now.

The Lakota shaman nodded to me before he spoke. "Tell him

53

that you have the gift. Tell him his grandmother had dreams often as well."

I discreetly shook my head, not wanting to get hauled off and detained because an FBI agent thought I was totally crazy or stalking his grandmother. There had to be some sort of post-9/11 anti-terrorism laws enacted that would have covered a case like that.

"Mrs. Baker, I asked you a question." Agent Oliver's demanding voice cut into my thoughts.

"I'm sorry. Could you repeat that please?"

"I said, is this something that happens to you often? Getting information about crimes? In other words, do you believe you are some sort of psychic?"

"To be honest with you, Agent Oliver . . . yes, I suppose I do. This type of gift seems to run in my family." I paused, weighing my next words carefully and trying to ignore the knot growing in my stomach. "Just like it does in yours."

The large man paused, a flicker of something—I wasn't sure exactly what—flashed across his steal gray eyes. "I see." He returned the notebook to his breast pocket. "I'll be in touch, Mrs. Baker. And if you have any more . . . dreams . . . I'd appreciate it if you'd let me know."

I stood up, prepared to see him out. Without waiting for me, the law enforcement officer headed to the door and walked out. Unfortunately, the heavy feeling he brought with him didn't leave at the same time.

10

I had learned my lesson the first time. Right after dinner while still sitting at the table, as Zach, Madison and Mackenzie were playing in their rooms, I told Matt about the afternoon's visitor.

"Do you think you should get a lawyer?" Concern saturated his voice. "I mean, do you think he's going to arrest you? You didn't do it, did you?"

"Matt! How could you think that?"

"Just tell me you didn't. Remember, I'm an insecure man," he said, alluding to a long-standing joke between the two of us.

"Of course I didn't do it." I pushed my plate toward the middle of the table and leaned my elbows on the deep, polished mahogany. "I just wish I hadn't called that tip line, to be honest."

Matt leaned back in his chair, looking as relaxed as if he'd just eaten a Thanksgiving meal. In reality, it had been a dinner of Gypsy Casserole and a salad with Ginger Vinaigrette dressing, a meal my mother had made when I was growing up. "I'm sure you do. But it's not that big of a deal. Cerri, I knew you were . . . talented . . . before we got married. I also knew you had a strong sense of justice and right." He leaned forward and grabbed my hand in his. "Those are some of the reasons I love you. I'd be disappointed if you didn't try to help in any way you could."

I looked into his eyes, hoping for additional reassurance. "Really?"

He lifted my hand to his lips, giving my fingers a light kiss before replying. "Yes. Really. I love you. The serious you, the funny you, the worrying you, the 'special' you. I love all of you." He waited only a moment for me to protest, which I almost did, before he continued in a more serious tone. "So, what do we do now?"

"I have no idea," I sighed. "This is all new to me."

"Well, I hate to bring it up, but has anything like this ever happened to your mom or sister? One of them might be able to give you some pointers."

This time I really did have to protest. "No! I am not going to ask one of them what to do when the FBI shows up on the front porch again. You have got to be kidding." I stood and started clearing away the dishes.

Matt followed, also grabbing dirty plates and glasses and

carrying them into the kitchen. "No, babe, I'm serious. Your mom may have helped the authorities at some point and can tell you what you should do next. You have to admit, this really is more her and your sister's realm than it is yours or mine."

Okay, so Matt had a point.

When we finished with the dishes, I decided it would be as good a time as any to call my mother. Maybe Matt was right and she'd be able to give me some advice on what to next. At the very least she had more experience dealing with the mystical side of life then I did. I dialed Mother's number and she answered on the first ring.

"Hi, Ma. How's everything there?" I knew I was stalling, but I couldn't see just jumping in with the reason why I'd really called.

"Here? Everything's fine. There? You have problems." Her Irish lilt held a touch of humor that told me she had been expecting my call.

I wasn't going to give in that easily, though. "Problems? What makes you say that?"

Mother laughed, but ignored my question. "So what's the problem, my love? What is causing you to have such distress?"

That was all it took. Despite my previous resolve, the floodgates opened and I told her everything that had happened. When I'd finished, I took a deep breath and asked, "So what do I do now? That FBI guy thinks I had something to do with the killing and the ghost thinks I can help find the murderer!"

"Oh my dear," Mother started, her tone calmly reassuring, "you have been called."

"What? I don't understand."

"While you were speaking, I drew a card for you. You haven't done that yet, have you?"

Feeling like a small child who forgot to finish her chores, I admitted that I hadn't touched a tarot deck in months—if not years.

"Well, dear, that should have been your first reaction. You are good with the cards and they speak to you. But no matter, I drew one for you."

Tarot cards have always been a staple in Mother's home. I'm sure Dad never picked up a deck on his own, but she consulted them for every major life decision. She also did annual birthday readings for Wendy and me while we were growing up. It didn't surprise me that Mother would have drawn a card while I was talking to her.

"Really? You drew a card for me? Wonderful." I tried to keep the sarcasm out of my voice. I really did want her help, but somehow I wasn't as excited about Mother drawing a tarot card for me as I was at the prospect of her giving me tips on getting out of this jam I currently found myself in.

I vaguely wondered if the card would tell me how to deal with Agent Oliver.

"Mind your manners, lass. I drew the Eight of Pentacles. Do you remember what that means?"

"Pentacles are the earth cards, they usually mean money and health. The eights are strength." I was stalling, and Mother knew it.

"Yes, yes. Now what does that card mean? Spit it out, Cerridwen."

"All right. It means that a new move could cause a major identity shift and that there is enough strength to step up to the challenge." Even I could hear the defeated tone in my voice. Thankfully, Mother chose to ignore it. In the next room, Matt turned up the television's volume enough to hint that he was trying to drown me out.

"Very good, dear. So I take this to mean that your move to the Black Hills is a good one for you. Your first mission, of course, is to help solve this murder."

Exasperated, I asked, "And just how am I supposed to do that? I just told you this FBI agent thinks I had something to do with a murder! How am I supposed to step up to a challenge I don't even want when I can't get people to believe me in the first place?"

Mother sighed. It was a sound I was used to, since I was often the cause of her frustration. "There will be a way to share the information. The Universe would not entrust it to you if there was nothing you could do."

"I understand that. I don't like it, but I understand." There was a short pause before I continued. "So what do I do? How do I tell the FBI agent anything else and have him believe me? Ma, I really need your advice here. In plain English, preferably."

"You'll just have to be persistent. Look for an opening and you will find a way. Use the things you've been taught, Cerridwen."

"Gee, thanks for the advice," I wanted to say. Instead, I changed the subject, asking Mother about her day. We talked for a few more minutes before saying our goodbyes.

After hanging up the phone, I sulked into the living room where Matt was flipping channels.

"How'd it go? Any good advice?"

I know he was only trying to help, but I couldn't even answer him. Matt must have picked up on my not-so-subtle non-verbal cues, though.

"That bad, huh?" He raised one eyebrow as he asked the

question. "Sorry, babe. I thought for sure your mom could help."

Plopping into the nearest recliner I replied, "I'm sure she could have helped—if she'd wanted to. Wasn't something she felt like doing."

"Wanna talk about it?" Matt's words were right, but the underlying tone of his voice practically begged me to say no.

I pacified him. "I'm sure I'll find an answer in the morning."

Suddenly I was very tired and wanted nothing more than the sweet respite of a good night's sleep. Deep down, however, I wasn't sure I'd ever be able to sleep again without being haunted by visions of FBI agents hunting me down for murders I had nothing to do with.

11

It had been a long time since Matt and I had been out on a date. We tried to spend some kid-free time together each month but, since Matt had moved to South Dakota two months before the rest of the Baker clan, we hadn't had the chance lately. I was especially looking forward to the evening.

The neighbor girls arrived promptly at five o'clock. The kids had been told to behave and the babysitters were given all the important numbers and Matt and I were ready to go by a quarter after. We climbed into Matt's Saturn and headed toward Rapid City.

The road into Rapid followed the terrain well—mostly hills and curves. Even though the grass was more brown than green, the vibrant reds and yellows of leaves still clinging to the trees made it a scenic drive. While Matt drove, we sat in comfortable silence.

I took a deep breath, closing my eyes as I inhaled, the scent of Matt's aftershave mixing with the vanilla-cardboard odor of the cheap air freshener hanging from the rearview mirror. I sat that way for a few minutes, listening to the radio and feeling the tension in my shoulders melt with each rotation of the tires. When I opened my eyes, I saw we were much closer to the city than I had anticipated. Houses and stoplights would soon replace the trees as scenery.

I heard my stomach growl. I hadn't realized how hungry I was. "Where are we going for dinner? I'm starving."

"We're going to—"

He didn't have a chance to finish. He swerved to the right, as a large white-tail buck darted in front of us. I screamed and felt the car leave the road. I was momentarily grateful not to hear the crunch of metal and knew Matt hadn't hit the animal.

My relief was short lived.

Instead of the smooth pavement, we were now bouncing down an embankment, headed toward a line of trees.

Matt yelled a curse word.

I forced my head to the left, trying to catch a glimpse of Matt. Would he get us back on the road? The grass made odd scraping noises at it brushed the underside of the vehicle.

I screamed again as tree branches scraped the roof and sides of the car. I could feel myself tense up more than I had in a long time. I looked up in time to see a large oak right in front of us. Matt was twisting the wheel hard.

The crunch of the car hitting the tree was overshadowed only by the jolt of our sudden stop and the loud explosion that followed. I was aware of hitting the window moments before the tree shattered it, raining glass down on me. The smell of sulfur assaulted me. My ears were ringing and I assumed the air bag had deployed.

We were finally stopped.

"Cerri! Cerri! Are you okay?" Matt was yelling, grabbing my hand. He sounded so far away.

"I . . . I think so. Are you?"

He ignored my question. "Cerri, you're bleeding. Where are you hurt?"

I reached up and touched my right temple. The warm, thick, stickiness on my fingers confirmed I had some kind of a cut. Since the sight of blood usually makes me sick, I rubbed my hand against my jacket to keep from seeing any more.

Matt unbuckled his seat belt and got out of the car. He half-walked, half-ran around to my side of the car, slapping his palm against the trunk on the way.

"Cerri," he yelled, "don't move, honey. Your door is pretty bashed in. I know I can't get it open. Stay calm, sweetie." Matt's voice cracked as he tried to remain calm. He's never been a very good actor.

I heard Matt talking to someone, so I assumed he called nine-one-one.

"They'll be here soon, honey." Matt had walked back to the driver's side of the car and was trying to hold my hand through the mess.

I wanted to get out and stand next to him, but wasn't sure I could. It had taken me a few minutes, but I finally realized my right leg was pinned. I vaguely wondered if I was in shock and then remembered reading that if I *were* in shock, I probably wouldn't know it. That's the same logic that says crazy people don't know they're insane. It may have been flawed logic, but it worked for me at the moment.

Sirens sounded in the distance. They were coming closer and I hoped they would hurry. My leg was starting to really hurt, but I wasn't sure if the pain was real or imagined.

More than anything, I wanted to go home and hug the kids.

I leaned my head back and closed my eyes.

"It's okay, ma'am, we're going to get you out of there." The deep voice belonged to an older man in a paramedic's uniform with the most impressive blue eyes I'd ever seen. I'm not sure about the rest of him, but his eyes looked almost neon. It was something different to focus on. "Can you tell me where you're hurt?"

"I don't know. I can't move my leg. It's pinned in." I tried hard to keep the panic out of my voice. I wanted to make a joke, but couldn't think of anything funny about the situation. "Just get me out," I begged.

The paramedic started an IV through the driver's side of the wrecked car and mentioned something about morphine before I just didn't care what happened anymore.

~~~~~

I awoke in a hospital bed, the IV still attached to my arm. Groggily I rubbed my eyes, wondering where my clothes were and why I was wearing the gown.

An overly cheerful, grandmotherly nurse entered the room. "Mrs. Baker. How are you? Feeling better, my dear? You have a visitor!"

"Um . . . a visitor? What time is it? Why am I here?"

"Oh, honey, you were in a car accident. Don't you remember?" Concern clouded her face as she checked readouts on various machines. I thought I even smelled a hint of sugar cookie as she leaned over me. "You have a bit of a concussion, and needed some stitches in your head. You have a bad sprain in your ankle. Lots of bumps and bruises from that accident!"

The nurse stuck a thermometer in my mouth before I could say anything. As soon as it came out, I started bombarding her with questions.

"How's Matt? Is he okay? Who's the visitor? Matt? Where is he? What time is it? When can I go home?"

The nurse started to answer, but the opening of the hospital room door interrupted her.

"Well. You're finally awake."

I recognized the voice of Special Agent Oliver and briefly wondered how much worse things could possibly get.

"No. I'm tired and want to go back to sleep. Thanks for stopping by." The nurse snickered as she left the room and I wondered how much charm had to be lacking in the man for the Mrs. Claus of the nursing world to have disliked him.

"Nice try, Mrs. Baker. I have a few questions for you."

"Look, Agent Oliver. It's been a really long day . . . or night, whatever it is. I'm not sure I have anything to say. I don't have anything to add about the death, and I surely don't know anything about the deer that attacked us on the road. If my husband is okay,

I'd like to rest."

"Your husband is fine. In fact, he's down in the cafeteria getting a cup of coffee." For a second, I thought I detected kindness in the FBI agent's voice, but it was probably a hallucination thanks to the really good drugs they had given me.

Agent Oliver continued. "Now, I have some additional questions for you."

"Fine," I said, rolling my eyes, an involuntary movement that I didn't think would have hurt. I was wrong. It hurt a lot.

Agent Oliver pulled his notebook out of the breast of his suit jacket and I wondered for a moment if he always wore suits.

Yep, really good drugs. "Why are you even here? Why would the FBI care about us hitting a tree?"

"You don't remember?" Agent Oliver studied me carefully; using the same look I've seen my geologist husband use to study rocks. "You said some interesting things while you were out of it. One of the nurse's aids called us."

I didn't remember much of anything since the paramedic started the IV in the car. I certainly didn't remember talking to nurses or saying things that would prompt them to call the FBI. He must have deduced as much from my blank stare.

"You claimed to know who killed Scott Curtis. You gave a description of a woman and even some interesting theories about the crime. In addition, you said you knew why he as killed at Devils Tower." Agent Oliver paused, intently watching my face to see what kind of reaction his words were having on me. "It was enough to have this nurse think you must be involved. Frankly, I think she's right. I just can't prove it. Yet."

"I don't care what you think." I was tired and in pain and worried about Matt and the kids and couldn't imagine the conversation ending well. Actually, I couldn't imagine the conversation ending any way other than me in jail.

"You will." All traces of humanity had once again left the FBI agent and his inner jerk returned to the surface. "Now, what *exactly* do you know about the murder of Scott Curtis."

"I don't know anything. Honest." I sounded like one of the kids trying to get out of trouble. "I really don't. I only know what I've already told you."

"So this nurse was making it all up? You don't know anything and what you do know came in a dream. Yeah, right."

Despite the return of the jackhammer in my head, I wanted to argue with the badge-toting idiot. Like I was going to lie to him. The most trouble I'd ever been in before was a speeding ticket, although a few too many of those, maybe. I opened my mouth to tell Agent Oliver exactly where he could go with his innuendo, when the door to the hospital room opened again.

Matt walked in carrying two steaming Styrofoam cups. My knight in shining armor had rescued me once again—this time from saying anything I might later regret.

"Hey, Joe. The nurse told me you were in here and that Cerri was awake." Matt handed Agent Oliver one of the cups before heading to the bed and planting a kiss on my forehead.

Speechless, I briefly contemplated turning away from my traitor husband's kiss, but I remembered how rolling my eyes hurt and thought better of it. How Matt could make friends with the enemy was something he would have to explain later. In detail.

"Matt. I was just asking your wife here what she knew about my case."

"Was she any help?" The two men acted as if I wasn't even there.

"No. But I didn't expect her to be."

"News flash. I'm in the same room as the two of you." My Irish temper, another trait I'd inherited from my mother, hit its flashpoint. I wasn't sure if I was more upset with the FBI agent for being in my room, or with Matt for seeming to have made friends with the enemy.

I caught the slightest look of amusement cross Matt's face as he continued toward the chair near my bed. He made himself comfortable, ready to watch the exchange experience told him would follow.

"I don't know what you expect, *Special Agent Oliver*, but I've told you everything I know. I had nothing to do with your case. I don't know who the hell killed the guy. I mean I'm sorry he's dead and all, but I do *not* know who killed him."

"Mrs. Baker, you know information about this case that no one else knows. You knew the name of the victim before it was released to the public. All the evidence points to you knowing more than you're saying." The agent's voice was quiet and determined. I could only imagine the effect the combination of his stature and cool demeanor must have on those who were guilty of some crime.

"No good deed goes unpunished, right?" I was only slightly shocked at the flippant tone of my voice. "Next time I have information that might help I'll keep it to myself."

The glare I received from the FBI agent would have made an

Eskimo shiver. "Really? So there will be a next time, Mrs. Baker?" I opened my mouth to speak again, when he cut me off. "I'm sure you'd like to rest now. I'll be back in the morning. Nice meeting you, Mr. Baker."

Without another word, the agent turned on his heels and left the room.

Matt shook his head in bewilderment. "Cerri, what have you gotten yourself into?"

Truthfully, I wondered the same thing. Again.

12

Hospitals are no place to actually rest. Machines beep and nurses come in the room to check on you often. Official sounding voices announce the need for various staff through a public address system and new arrivals make their appearance with the clanging of gurneys and a team of assistants.

No, hospitals are no place for real rest.

Unless, of course, you are the mother of three children all under the age of eight.

Despite the activity, I awoke as refreshed as could be. One of the night nurses had told me there would be another set of x-rays for my leg and I might be released by the early afternoon.

Since the swelling seemed to have diminished, and the pain had decreased to only a dull ache, I was hopeful I'd be home by dinner. Midmorning, a nurse took me to the x-ray department. When I returned, I heard Agent Oliver's gruff voice coming from my room. He sounded less happy than usual.

"Hold on a second," I whispered to the orderly. We stopped just outside the door, where I could here Agent Oliver's ranting. I wasn't in any hurry to speak with him—especially if I was right about his mood.

"With me, sir? As in helping with this investigation?"

He paused and I figured he must be speaking to someone on the phone.

"But, sir! She's a *civilian!*" He said the last word like it was a poison. "Yes, sir. I understand, sir."

Another pause. The orderly was getting a little antsy and I wasn't sure how much longer he'd wait outside my room.

"Just another second. Please?" I whispered, practically begging him.

"Yes, sir. I'll explain the situation to her as soon as possible. For the record, though, I do—"

I'd never heard Agent Oliver so polite before and assumed that he was talking to his boss. I couldn't imagine him speaking that respectfully to anyone else.

"Yes, sir. I understand, sir." There was the telltale snap of a flip phone shutting. "Damn!"

I sheepishly looked up at the orderly. "I guess we can go in now."

The angry lawman turned to face us as the orderly wheeled me into the room. If I had thought Agent Oliver never looked pleasant before, whatever expression he held now was far worse. I was glad I wouldn't have to spend any length of time with the man. Whoever he had been talking about on the phone was definitely on the agent's "least favorite people of all time" list.

Although I didn't think it possible, his face clouded even more when he saw me. He didn't speak, but I could see the muscles of his jaw contracting as he gritted his teeth.

The orderly helped me get situated and left, saying as few words as possible. Through it all, the FBI agent didn't speak. He only clenched and unclenched his jaw, his steel gray eyes flashing with each muscle movement.

Once we were alone, however, Agent Oliver wasted no time.

"I don't know who you know," he started, "or why they seem to think you'd be helpful, but it won't work. You must have pulled some serious strings, Mrs. Baker, but my opinion of you has not changed. Not at all."

I no longer thought I was the crazy one. I now knew that this man had lost his marbles. "What are you talking about?"

"I'm supposed to forget that *you* are a suspect in this murder and you are now going to be working with me." Agent Oliver stared at me showing no more emotion than the granite faces South Dakota is so well known for. "I don't know who you've fooled, but rest assured it isn't me."

"What are you talking about?" I asked again. "I think you've lost it."

"You know what I'm talking about! I just got off the phone with my supervisor. According to him, you are going to work with me to solve the Scott Curtis murder." Agent Oliver paused, watching me intently as if trying to gauge my reaction. Unfortunately, I still had no idea what he was talking about.

The blank look on my face must have been convincing, because he continued.

"And *that* order came from someone in the CIA who had heard about your involvement in the case." He looked at me accusingly.

If I had been a cartoon character, a light bulb would have appeared over my head at that moment. Without a doubt, I knew exactly who had decided I needed to be involved with this.

Mother.

I rolled my eyes and leaned back into the bed. The obvious

scenario played out in my mind. Mother had told Dad about the case and my phone call. Dad, who did some type of top-secret work for the spy agency, apparently decided to placate Mother by getting the FBI agent off my back the easiest way he knew. Or else he really did think I could help solve a murder, in which case maybe he wasn't such a good top-secret spy type after all.

"Look, there's been a misunderstanding."

"Really? Why don't you try and explain it to me then, Mrs. Baker?"

I opened my mouth and it occurred to me that there really was no explanation, at least not one that sounded reasonable. Somehow I didn't think saying "My dad was just trying to help" would work.

"I'm waiting." Agent Oliver's voice returned to its usual warm and cheery tone, making stainless steel seems warm and inviting.

"Yeah, uh, I'm really not sure what to say. I think I know who called your boss, but I wouldn't venture to guess why."

"Care to enlighten me?"

"I'd rather have a little more information first. I'll make some calls when I get out of here and will let you know what I find out." Mentally I made a note to call Mother and find out what exactly she was thinking and how I could get out of my latest predicament.

"Fine," came the curt reply. "Until then, why don't you start by telling me everything you know?"

I wasn't going to fall for that line, since Agent Oliver and I had been over this before. I'd already told him what little information He Who Waits had bothered to show me. There was nothing else to share.

Thankfully, before I could speak the doctor walked into the room.

He was older, grandfatherly really, but had an ageless personality. He seemed to have learned his bedside manner in an age before HMOs forced doctors to see and treat as many patients as possible in as short a time as possible. Something told me he would be equally good with Matt's ninety-two year-old grandmother as he would be with Madison or Mackenzie.

"Well, young lady, I think you're free to go," he said, flipping through pages in my medical chart. "I can't find any reason to keep you here. How are you feeling? No blurred vision?"

I assured the doctor I was fine as he checked my eyes and other vital signs.

"Then I think you'll get more rest at home." He turned to the stoic man standing at the foot of my bed. "Make sure she gets plenty of rest, Mr. Baker. The nurse will be in with discharge papers soon."

"He's not my hus—" I started.

"I'll see that she gets plenty of rest, doctor," the FBI agent answered.

After the doctor left the room, I exploded.

"*You'll* see that I get plenty of rest? I think not!" I reached for the phone to call Matt.

"Relax, Mrs. Baker. I'm here and we've already established that we will be working together for the time being. I might as well give you a ride home."

Agent Oliver's almost human-like tone confused me. "I don't want to work with you."

"Well, the feeling is mutual," he admitted. "But right now I can't control it. When I prove you had something to do with Scott Curtis's murder, though, I'll know exactly where you are to arrest you."

This was getting worse and worse all the time.

13

The drive back to Cogan Ridge was quiet, neither Agent Oliver nor myself wanting to break the silence. I don't know what he was stewing about, but I was imagining the phone call I'd make to my parents.

Agent Oliver may not understand what I was doing mixed up in this investigation, but I knew perfectly well who was responsible for this predicament. I called her Ma. The only reasonable explanation to my current situation was that she had told Dad to intervene.

My father spent thirty-five years working in Army intelligence. When he retired as a four-star general, he decided he was too young to not head to the office. So, even though he and Mother didn't need the money, he went to work for the state department. I didn't ask what he did—he hadn't been able to tell me for most of my life anyway.

I didn't believe it was a coincidence that right after I called Mother looking for a way to get Agent Oliver to believe me, he was ordered to work with me on the case. That was something Mother would have enjoyed talking Dad into.

"Hello. Did you hear me, Mrs. Baker?" Agent Oliver's deep voice brought me back to the present.

"No, sorry. And you might as well call me Cerri if we're going to be stu—working together."

"I think you were right the first time. 'Stuck' together is more appropriate." We had reached the subdivision and I was grateful to realize we'd be at my house in just a few more minutes.

"I asked if you had any new insight," the agent repeated.

"No, I don't. I've told you everything I know."

Agent Oliver snorted. "Somehow, I doubt that."

We pulled into my driveway and I began getting out of the car. I probably started to leave before he even had the car in park, but I didn't care. From inside the house, I could hear the kids laughing. Suddenly I wanted nothing more than to be with them.

For the millionth time, I regretted making the "anonymous" phone call that got me involved with this mess.

"Look, Cerri," Agent Oliver started, stopping me from actually exiting the vehicle, "I won't lie. I don't want to be working with you, but I don't have a choice. My bosses say I have to and that order is coming down from somewhere higher up. There's nothing I can do about it."

"It's not my id—"

He continued as if I hadn't spoken. "I'm going to find out who killed Scott Curtis. I'm also going to find out why I've been ordered to baby-sit you while I do it. I don't even know what they think you can bring to the investigation."

I didn't think he was finished yet, so I glared at him, waiting for him to go on. For an instant, I considered telling him who had given the order but then decided keeping that information from him might be more fun for me. I let my devilish side win.

"Be at the Federal Building on Saint Joseph first thing Monday morning. Number four hundred. We'll go interview Scott's co-workers."

I finished getting out of the car. "Fine. I'll see you then." I slammed the door with more force than necessary and headed toward the house. It took all my effort not to limp on my still-sore leg. At least it wasn't broken, only sprained and bruised. There was something to be thankful for.

Once inside the house, I was greeted to screams of "Mommy" and "Mommy's home." There was even a banner the kids had decorated hanging on the wall. They had raided my printer paper and found enough scotch tape to make the seven-foot-long sign. It looked like they had used every crayon in their vast collection, as well.

It was the most beautiful thing I'd ever seen.

I spent the rest of the day with four servants at my beck and call. I wasn't allowed to lift even one finger. Madison and Mackenzie brought me glasses of water and all the books and magazines they could find. Zach brought cookies to me every few minutes, often with crumbs on his own face.

Matt was the most attentive—partially, I think, because he felt responsible for the accident.

"Sweetheart, it wasn't your fault," I said when I finally got him alone. "That deer came out of nowhere."

Matt looked at the ground.

"There's a reason they call them accidents, you know," I continued.

"You could have been seriously hurt, Cerri. Hell, you could have been killed!"

"But I wasn't. I don't blame you and I wish you wouldn't either."

He didn't answer. I hadn't expected him to. One of the things I loved most about Matt was his sensitivity. It was also one of the things about him that drove me the most crazy.

"Oh! I forgot to tell you."

"Tell me what?" Matt looked skeptically at me.

"I'll be working with that FBI agent now."

"Yeah, right. I got the impression he didn't like you much."

I told Matt what had transpired at the hospital and on the drive home. "So, this you *can* take credit for. If you hadn't suggested I call Mother, she wouldn't have told Dad and I wouldn't be in this mess."

A look of relief passed over Matt's face. "That's why you didn't call me? Because he was already there to interview you again? I thought you were so mad you didn't want to ride in the car with me again."

Sometimes Matt was just too sensitive.

"You're kidding, right?" I could see he wasn't kidding. "I would have much rather you came for me, but I wasn't sure how to get out of the ride with Agent Oliver. Just like I'm not sure how to avoid having to work with him."

"Well that makes me feel better." He kissed me, then a mischievous grin spread across his face. "Although, I wouldn't want you be your mom the next time you talk to her."

14

Monday morning found me still sore, but I didn't think that was reason enough to cancel the appointment with Agent Oliver. I was pretty sure I couldn't get out of it that easy.

After dropping the kids off at the bus stop, I headed into to Rapid City to meet the agent. He was waiting on the corner of Ninth Street and St. Joseph Avenue, his dark blue suit clearly pegging him as either FBI or accountant.

I found a parking spot near where he was standing. Before I could get out, though, the agent appeared at my driver's side door.

"Park in there," he said, pointing to the parking garage attached to the building. "Here's your pass. I'll meet you back here."

The man was his usual, pleasant self.

I took the credit card-sized piece of plastic and headed into the parking garage. A few moments later I was back at the corner, waiting to hear what we were doing next.

"We'll take my car." The large man led the way to a non-descript gray sedan. For a moment I wondered what other movie-stereotypes were accurate about the FBI. I wasn't sure I wanted to know, though, since I didn't like Agent Oliver and he obviously didn't like me. He intimidated the hell out of me, so I wasn't going to argue over who should drive.

Once in the car, the agent proceeded to act as if I wasn't there. He didn't say anything as he started the vehicle and pulled out into traffic. As the silence stretched to uncomfortable lengths, I began to fiddle with my hands. I didn't want to be here and Agent Oliver wasn't making this any easier. I reminded myself to call my mother when I returned home from this torturous adventure. I had successfully avoided talking to her since my release from the hospital, but she still had some explaining to do.

Lost in my own thoughts, I hadn't noticed the car had stopped. We were in a bowling alley parking lot. Before I could ask anything, Mr. Personality started barking orders.

"You won't say anything. You won't ask any questions. You will do what I tell you, when I tell you to do it." His voice was flat; his tone even more intimidating than usual. "Don't screw this up for me or I will charge you with obstruction of justice. And no one will be able to get you out of it."

"Fine," I replied, trying to sound braver and more confident than I felt. "Will you at least tell me what's going on?"

He sighed. "We're about to go where our victim worked. Right now we don't have a lot of clues, which is why you're here. From what I understand, you're some kind of journalist and body language expert and are supposed to help me figure out who's lying."

That was the best Mother could come up with? Body language expert? Did such a profession even exist?

I took a deep, cleansing breath.

Body language expert I was not, but even I could tell Agent Oliver didn't believe the line he'd been given. I knew I'd have to not only follow his rules, but at the same time come up with something that would help the FBI investigation.

Talk about pressure.

"Okay. Let's do this." I hoped my voice didn't betray my nervousness.

Agent Oliver pulled back into traffic, drove less than two blocks, and turned into another parking lot.

The Peterson Construction offices were located near the western edge of Rapid City on Sturgis Road. Two large buildings—one I assumed to be offices, the other looked more like a storage facility—bore the company logo. There were only a handful of cars in the parking lot and I wondered where all the other cars were. Even having just moved to the area, the numerous trucks and other heavy equipment with the Peterson Construction name couldn't escape my attention.

I followed Agent Oliver into the closer of the two buildings, the one I assumed to house the main offices. Inside was decorated in the tans and beiges of Corporate America. There was the distinct smell of disinfectant, covered by air freshener and recycled air.

"Can I help you?" The woman at the counter had a high-pitched voice that reminded me of nails on a chalkboard. I was instantly grateful I didn't have to listen to that all day.

Agent Oliver reached into the breast pocket of his suit coat and pulled out his credentials. "Special Agent Joseph Oliver, FBI. We have an appointment with Mark Peterson."

The woman eyed me coolly, seeming to wonder who I was and why I wasn't introduced. She struck me more like a jealous lover than the company receptionist.

"I'll let Mr. Peterson know you're here," she finally responded when it seemed obvious that she wasn't going to get an answer to her unasked questions. When she spoke I noticed a faint accent, German or Croatian maybe?

She stood, smoothing her too-tight business skirt over her athletic figure. In her stiletto heels, she looked to be about my height of five-foot-nine. Her bleach-blonde hair was shoulder length and the dark roots proclaimed it was about time for another trip to the beauty parlor. She was very tan, and would have looked more at home in a bikini on the beach than she did sitting behind the desk.

I again had the thought that she didn't act much like a receptionist, although she may have looked the sexist stereotype. Glancing at the top of her desk, I noticed there wasn't much in the way of personal effects, nor were there the papers and files that covered my work area at home. There was a Dictaphone machine and I assumed she did most of her work straight on the state-of-the-art desktop computer. A jar of pens, most bearing the Peterson Construction name, a message pad, and a nameplate engraved with the name ELKE THOMPSON were the only other things on the desk. A plant took up residence on one of the filing cabinets which lined the far wall.

"Mr. Peterson, there's an FBI agent to see you." Her shrill announcement wasn't meant to be that loud, but I didn't think she could help it. It surprised me that I could think of her voice as both shrill and guttural and decided her accent must be German after all.

When she returned to her desk a few moments later, she was followed by an older gentleman I presumed to be Mark Peterson. Tall and tanned, he looked to be in his mid-fifties. He wore the business casual look favored by the upper management in a blue-collar field. He had a muscular build, but I felt it was from the gym and not the day-to-day construction work his employees performed.

"Hi. I'm Mark Peterson. How can I help you?" The man's voice was quiet and reserved. The closer he got, the more powerful he seemed.

"Mr. Peterson, we're here with the FBI and I'd like to ask you a few questions."

If either the construction mogul or the over-sexed receptionist noticed how it was implied that only the man next to me would be asking questions, neither one mentioned it.

"Please, follow me." Mr. Peterson started back down the hallway. "Elke, hold my calls please."

"Yes, Mr. Peterson," the receptionist answered.

We followed the owner into his office. It was spacious, even with the large mahogany desk and overstuffed executive chair. Decorated in a style that could only be referred to as expensive, the room featured a mini-bar against one wall, while another was made up of floor-to-ceiling windows that looked out onto the hills. A door, discretely hidden on a third wall must have led to a boardroom area where the major wheeling-and-dealing of the company took place.

"Thank you for taking the time to see us, Mr. Peterson," began Agent Oliver.

"Please, call me Mark. What can I do for you?" Peterson gestured at a small sitting area I hadn't noticed before. The chairs and small couch looked inviting, even cozy, causing me to wonder what business activities a construction company owner would conduct there.

"Sir, we're investigating the death of one of your employees, a Scott Curtis."

"Tragic. Just tragic. Scott was a great guy. Wonderful employee." Peterson leaned against the arm of one of the chairs. I sat on the couch while the FBI agent copied the older man's pose.

"Tell me what Scott was like, please." Agent Oliver used his talent of turning a question into an order, but it didn't seem to faze Peterson.

"He was young, full of life. He'd only been working here about eighteen months or so, but I had no complaints."

"What exactly did he do?"

Peterson sighed. "He was a junior accountant. Scott handled the receivables. He was a great worker. Real asset come tax time. He'll be difficult to replace."

I wasn't sure what I was supposed to be learning from Mark Peterson. He seemed extremely confident, but I was nervous as heck. In college I'd taken classes in both psychology and sociology, and had been fascinated with body language. I searched my memory for the telltale clues of deception. The construction company CEO didn't seem to be hiding anything, at least not that I could tell.

I silently cursed Mother—again—for getting me into this mess.

Agent Oliver's booming voice brought my focus back on their conversation. "Did Scott have any enemies that you know of? Anyone who would want to do him harm?"

The older man smiled wanly. "I'm afraid I wouldn't really know anything about that. Like I said, Scott only started here about eighteen months ago as a junior accountant. I wasn't his direct boss. Our head accountant may know more, or probably one of the other juniors."

"I see. What about clients? Can you think of any business reasons why Scott could have been murdered?"

Peterson's laugh filled the room. While I'm sure he meant the sound to be jovial, to me it sounded forced and slightly corrupt.

"This is South Dakota, Agent Oliver," he finally said. "There's no big mob-boss in the construction business here. Do some of my business associates begrudge me my success? I'm sure they do. But this company was my father's before it was mine. We've been in business a long time. If Scott Curtis was murdered for business reasons, I can assure you it wasn't *my* business the killer was doing."

When he was finished, the older man watched the FBI agent carefully. Peterson's eyes narrowed and I thought I saw him clench his jaw. The cold stare between the two men seemed to drop the room's temperature.

I couldn't be sure if Peterson's reaction was in response to the question, or if the CEO was lying. Either way, I had the feeling he knew more than he cared to admit. Agent Oliver, though, seemed his usual charming self.

Peterson finally broke the silence. "Well, I sure do wish you luck in finding whoever did this." His good-ol'-boy demeanor was back in action. "I'm really sorry I couldn't be any more help."

"If you don't mind, Mr. Peterson, we'll talk to a few of Scott's co-workers. Possibly they can shed some more light on the situation."

"Sure, sure, no problem." Peterson walked over to his desk and pushed the intercom button. "Elke, show Agent Oliver and his assistant to accounting, please. Make sure Mike knows to answer any questions they have."

"Yes, Mr. Peterson," came the disembodied voice.

Turning his attention back to us, Peterson stuck out his hand. "Nice meeting you. Good luck with your investigation," he said, shaking hands with each of us as his secretary reached the door.

We exchanged pleasantries, then followed Elke down the hall. I wondered again why I was there since I seemed to have added nothing to the previous interview. I hoped that either Scott's coworkers would be more helpful or Agent Oliver would decide we were done and this experience would be over.

Elke silently led us down the hall, through the lobby and around to the other half of the building. This didn't feel as luxurious as Peterson's offices. The expensive framed prints gave way to more generic posters and the lush carpet was worn and ragged in some areas. It was obvious that the real work was done over here and most clients would never see this side of the building. I could see stairs ahead of us leading to a basement and wondered if that's where we headed. It wasn't.

About halfway down the hall, we stopped at a closed door. The plaque on the door read MICHAELA DAVIS, CPA. Without knocking, Elke led us into the office.

This area was more casual than Peterson's personal sanctuary had been, yet more cluttered than Elke's sparse desk. Photos of a boy and girl, both in their early teens, shared the desk with manila file folders and tax legers. The woman who seemed to inhabit the office was in her mid-forties and just starting to turn gray. Her mostly light-brown hair was tied in a loose bun and her hazel eyes held flicks of gold.

More casual in appearance, Michaela Davis didn't seem to have been expecting anyone in her offices. There were large three-ring binders on both of the chairs and a pile of papers sticking out of one of them. With her sleeves rolled up to the elbows, the CPA looked like she was comparing the two binders and adding pages to one, while sitting on the front edge of her desk.

Yep, now we're starting to get to where the work is really done.

"Ms. Davis, these people from the FBI would like to ask you a few questions," announced the secretary in her nails-on-the-chalkboard voice. "Mr. Peterson assured them they would have your full cooperation."

"Of course," Michaela replied, a momentary scowl crossing her brow. She picked up the binders and headed around the desk. "What can I do for you?"

While Agent Oliver explained why we were here, I thought back to the conversation we'd had with Peterson. He had called the head of accounting "Mike," an interesting nickname for a woman. While I was zoning out, Agent Oliver must have mentioned the same thing.

"Mr. Peterson and I go way back," Michaela replied. "I used to baby-sit his kids, even. He's called me 'Mike' since I was twelve."

"I see," Agent Oliver responded. "What can you tell us about Scott Curtis?"

Michaela looked at Agent Oliver, as if trying to anticipate the type of answer he was really looking for. "I guess I wouldn't really know," she replied. Her voice seemed to lose some of its jovial quality.

"Why not?"

"I didn't really know him that well. He worked for me, sure, but it's not like we socialized at all."

She was lying. I had a vision of Scott and Michaela at a club, drinking and dancing together. I didn't know where it came from, but there was no doubt in my mind that the two of them had at least socialized, if not dated.

"You never went out for drinks after work?" I asked, forgetting Agent Oliver's firm instructions to remain silent.

Michaela's eyes met mine with a glare usually reserved for small children. "No. Peterson Construction has a strict no-fraternization policy. I couldn't have gone out for drinks with Scott if I had wanted to."

After a warning look from the FBI agent, he continued his own line of questioning. "What was he like at work? Professional? Any resentment among other employees?"

"No, nothing. He really hadn't been here that long, only about eighteen months or so. I can look up his hire date if you'd like."

Clearly, Michaela was lying again. I didn't know why, but assumed it was to keep their relationship under wraps.

"Mr. Peterson said that Scott handled receivables. What does that entail?"

The CPA explained how the business books were handled in a brief Accounting 101 lecture.

"So here at Peterson Construction, Scott did receivables. Tom Kennedy sent out invoices and Scott recorded them." Michaela's eyes had the faint twinkle of someone discussing a favorite subject. "That's a fairly simplistic explanation, of course, but you get the idea."

All of this I remembered from my college days. Oliver, on the other hand, had been taking notes.

"And would that have made him any enemies?" The agent looked up from his pad of paper.

"Not likely," she replied. "Scott would only have dealt with receivables."

I glanced at Agent Oliver and thought I saw a blank look pass his face. It was the same look Matt gave me when I discussed the virtues of a new sewing machine. Michaela Davis must have noticed it as well.

"Since he only handled incoming money, there's not much chance he would have developed enemies. It's usually the ones who owe us money who get upset, and that would have been the collections guys," the accountant said. "Even Tom had a better chance of making enemies since he's the one who sent the bills."

"Tom? That would be the Tom Kennedy you mentioned earlier." Two points for Agent Obvious.

"Right," Michaela agreed. "Scott and Tom really worked the two sides of the same accounts."

A thought occurred to me. "Who gets Scott's job now? I mean, would there have been someone—some coworker, maybe—who profited by his death?"

Michaela looked thoughtfully for a moment before answering. "You know, we haven't filled that position yet. I do know that Mr. Peterson had Elke post the job on some online sites. I don't think we've even gotten any resumes in. I'll tell you, though, Scott will be hard to replace. He had a fantastic memory for numbers. Almost like that one disorder—you know, the one with that Tom Cruise and Dustin Hoffman movie?"

"Autism?" I asked.

"Yeah, that one." Michaela nodded. "You could show Scott a set of numbers and he would remember them forever."

Agent Oliver regained control of the interview. "Did Scott supervise anyone? Would there have been someone who could have been next in line for his position?"

"Not really," the CPA answered. "The junior accountants here are all pretty much on the same level. There are some seniority issues, but nothing else. Nothing like what you're talking about anyway."

"We're going to need to talk to Tom Kennedy." Another order, cleverly disguised as a statement, from the over-confident agent.

Michaela moved a stack of folders and looked at the large desk calendar that had been previously buried under them. "Sorry, he's not in today. Sick kid." She looked up. "Tell you what, why don't I give you his address and phone number and you can catch him at home. Would that work?"

The FBI Agent took the information and made some comments about being in touch. Like a lost puppy, I followed him out of the building.

Back in the car, my traveling companion regained the charm I'd come to expect.

"You were supposed to keep your mouth shut. Not ask questions." The under current in his voice was mildly frightening, but I was pretty sure FBI agents were forbidden from harming people forced to work with them.

At least I hoped they were.

"Well, I thought—"

"I don't care what you thought!" Agent Oliver paused, as he started the car. "Make no mistake, Mrs. Baker. I don't think you can add anything to this investigation. In fact, just the opposite."

What was I supposed to say to that? Rather than argue, or even assure him that I agreed, I said nothing. We sat in silence as the FBI agent maneuvered the non-descript sedan through traffic and toward Tom Kennedy's home.

We arrived at an older home off of West Boulevard. The well-maintained lawn fit in with the other older, yet well-kept homes lining the street. The house itself looked like it was built in the 1900s, with few changes to the outside.

Parking the car on the street, Agent Oliver snapped, "No talking. I mean it." He emphasized the order by slamming the car door as he got out.

I rolled my eyes as I exited the car. I wasn't going to purposely defy the federal agent, but I knew from experience that being silent was often harder than it sounded.

The cracked sidewalk leading up to the porch was lined with Fischer-Price toys, Hot Wheels, and Barbie Dolls, evidence of multiple children having hours of enjoyment. Once on the porch, the FBI agent's steps slowed. He twisted his head a bit, as if trying to hear what was going on inside the house. I recognized the sounds of a PBS children's show through the open door.

Agent Oliver rapped twice on the screen.

"Daddy, someone's at the door," came a barely audible reply.

No wonder he had stayed home, I thought. That child must have one of the worst sore throats ever.

Within seconds a man appeared at the screen door. "Can I help you?"

"Are you Tom Kennedy?" Agent Oliver was his usual pleasant self.

"Who wants to know?"

While Agent Oliver preformed the introductions, I studied the man on the other side of the screen. He appeared to be in his mid-thirties, his medium brown hair starting to thin at the top. His coffee-colored eyes were cautious, and the dark circles beneath them gave silent testimony to how tired he was. The sweatpants and T-shirt were rumpled, as if he'd slept in them.

After confirming his identity, Tom Kennedy invited us into his home. "Sorry, Sarah's been sick for a few days," he explained as he moved a laundry basket out of the way.

The FBI agent glared, but I said, "Don't worry. I've been there."

Those five words seemed to put Tom at ease. His shoulders sagged a bit and I could almost see the tension leave his face. "So, how can I help you?"

Agent Oliver went through his explanation again, and I watched

Tom for any non-verbal signals that might come in handy. He didn't seem surprised to see us but then he didn't seem overly nervous, either.

"I don't know what I can tell you. Hold on, a sec." Tom stuck his head in the next room. "You doing okay, Sarah?"

"Yes, Daddy," came the whispered reply.

While Tom was preoccupied with his daughter, Agent Oliver took the opportunity to shoot me another scowl. Although this one wasn't quite as menacing as previous glares.

"Let's go in the dining room." Tom led the way to what would have been a formal dining room in days gone by. Now it housed a state-of-the-art computer and a multitude of programs in addition to the four-person table and chair set.

We each took a cushion-covered wooden seat.

"Where was I?" Tom finally asked. "Oh, yeah. Like I said, I'm not sure what all I can tell you. Scott was a great guy, and it's a real tragedy what happened to him. I hope you find whoever did it."

Agent Oliver's steel grey eyes studied the tired homeowner. "How well did you know Scott?"

Tom rubbed the stubble on his chin. "Pretty well, I guess. As well as he let anyone get to know him. Scott was a really private person. He was pretty shy actually. But we worked together and played darts."

"Darts?" Not even Special Agent Personality could hide the surprise in his voice.

Tom chuckled. "Yeah. Pretty lame, I know, but we were on the same dart league."

"How did that come about?"

"Well, we'd been working together three or four months, I guess, and I was giving him a bad time about not having any kind of social life."

I tried to hide my chuckle, thinking Agent Oliver probably didn't have much of a social life either. I didn't succeed very well and earned yet another glare from the FBI agent. Sometimes my naturally sarcastic nature doesn't make it easy to work well with others.

Taking advantage of the break in Tom's narrative, Agent Oliver asked, "Who started working at Peterson Construction first?"

"I did," Tom answered. "I've been working there almost three years now."

"And you took Scott under your wing when he got there?" Agent Oliver's voice was practically dripping with cynicism.

"Well, not really," said Tom. "We worked the same accounts. In laymen's terms, I sent the bills out and he collected the money. We talked every day about those accounts. Personally, though, Scott was really private. Most of us in accounting would at least mention what we'd done over the weekend or what our plans were or what TV shows we watched even. You know, office talk. Not Scott. He never mentioned his free time. So one day, I started giving him a bad time about it. I asked him if he sat in his apartment staring at a blank wall until Monday morning came around."

Tom looked up, first at the FBI agent and then me, before continuing his story. "Anyway, we struck up a strange friendship. Eventually, he told me he liked to play darts. I've been in a league for years and Scott played a bit in college. So I asked him to join us. Every week we played at the Valley Sports Bar. That was over a year ago."

"What was Scott like to work with?" Agent Oliver asked while my gaze drifted around the room. From what I'd seen so far, police work was not nearly as exciting as those television dramas made it out to be. In fact, I was bored out of my mind.

Tom shrugged his shoulders as he spoke, as if trying to find the right words to describe his relationship with the dead man. "He was a real dependable worker, ya' know? The kind of guy you could ask to finish up a project and you know he'd have it done on time. And he probably wouldn't have told the boss he did the whole thing alone, either."

A fit of coughing erupted from the other room. Tom looked worriedly toward the sound. "Excuse me. I need to go check on her," he said, rising from the chair and heading out of the room.

Tom's departure made me realize how uncomfortable the chair really was. My leg was starting to ache from being banged up in the accident. I wriggled a little and stifled a yawn, causing Agent Oliver to shoot me a glare.

"You know he didn't do it," I hissed. "We're wasting his time—and ours."

Not surprisingly, I received another glare from Agent Jerk. I'm not sure what came over me, but I didn't take the hint.

"We aren't going to learn much from him," I continued.

"Really?" The sarcasm was thick in his voice. "And you would know this how?"

Tom's return stopped me from answering, although I really wanted to remind the idiot that I hadn't requested to be here—more like I was forced. Plus the chair was getting more uncomfortable by the minute, and I was starting to get more irritable by the minute.

Maybe there was a correlation.

Since I was in such a foul mood anyway, I opted to ignore Agent Oliver's authoritarian rule and ask some questions on my own. It's not like journalism and police interrogations were all that different.

"Tom, can you tell me if Scott was seeing anyone?" I tried to sound nonchalant, but the question sounded intrusive to me. I valued my privacy and didn't want to be forcing in on someone else's. I couldn't think of a better, or faster, way to get Tom to talk about his friend's private life, though.

Tom didn't seem to mind. His face visibly relaxed as he considered the question. "Yeah, I think he was, but I don't know who."

I looked quizzically at Tom while ignoring the disgusted snort coming from Agent Oliver.

"Like I said, Scott was real quiet, but something changed the last few months. He was more . . . relaxed, I guess is a good way to describe it." Tom paused again, as if searching for the correct words. I was reminded once again how feelings and emotions are so much easier for women to put into words then they are for men. "It's not like he was bragging about her or anything, but he had that look. The one a guy gets when he's finally found the one, and is getting ready to buy the ring, ya' know?"

I knew exactly what Tom meant, but Agent Oliver looked clueless. Oh, well. Let him figure it out on his own.

My smile was all the encouragement Tom needed to continue. "He had a few new sweaters and he seemed in a hurry to leave right away, not stay late and work. It was a good thing for him, but I don't know who the mystery woman was."

Another fit of coughs erupted from the next room. Agent Oliver and I said our goodbyes and turned to leave.

Once at the door, however, I stopped and faced Tom again. "Have you tried giving your daughter some tea? For her throat?"

"She has some cough medicine the doctor gave her."

"Try a peppermint tea. It will help."

Tom looked at me for a moment. "Um, thanks. I'll give it a try."

As Agent Oliver and I headed back to the car, the FBI agent glared at me once again. "I thought you were supposed to be quiet."

I shrugged. "Thought I could help. It's what I do."

I could have sworn I heard the deep chuckle of He Who Waits as I slammed the car door shut.

15

By the time I made it home, I wanted to lock myself in my office and do nothing. I was sure there was a box of books somewhere I hadn't actually read yet.

As I unlocked the front door, though, a familiar presence signaled I would not get my wish.

"You have learned much, *Cuwitku*. But you have not learned all." He Who Waits started speaking before I even stepped across the threshold.

"Geez! What more do you want from me? I've done the interviews and gave the information to that jerk," I yelled back. "I'm done playing cops and robbers. Let him do his job."

He Who Waits studied me closely. For a brief moment, I recognized my father's eyes in the ancient shaman's and wondered about the connection before I looked away.

"In this case, he can not do his job without you. Only you will be able to give him the missing pieces."

Without another glance at He Who Waits, I headed into the kitchen and poured myself a glass of ice water. I planned to use the diversion to avoid answering him in the hope that he would vanish again.

I couldn't get that lucky.

"There is more to the story, *Cuwitku*."

I set the glass on the counter. "Fine. What more is there? What else can I do for this guy?" Silently I added, what else can I do to get you off my back?

"You will know what to do when the time is right. For now, there are more people to talk to."

"Look, he doesn't have any family around here. We talked to his co-workers. No one knows this guy! He was a loner. Real quiet. Nothing stands out about him."

"No one can tell you as much about a person as they can, Cerridwen."

I stood straighter, snapping my head in the shaman's direction. "What?"

"No one can tell you as much about a person as they can. You will learn more about this man from the man himself."

I rolled my eyes and leaned back against the kitchen counter. "I have no idea what you're talking about."

He Who Waits got that annoyed look I'd come to know so well. "What are you?" he asked.

"What?" I didn't understand the question. "What am I? I'm a wife, a mom, a writer . . ."

"Yes. You are all that," the shaman replied, nodding. "And you are a sister, a daughter, a friend. You are also a seer, a consumer, a member of the community, a seamstress, a knitter, the list continues. Does any one of those titles fully describe you, *Cuwitku*? I do not think so. How can you know who Scott Curtis is if you only see one side of him?"

I couldn't think of a good argument, so I said nothing. For a moment I wasn't sure which was more draining—arguing with my mother or with He Who Waits. As long as my thoughts where on that path, I briefly wondered who would win an argument between He Who Waits and Mother. I couldn't help but chuckle.

"You are learning," came the shaman's reply.

Did he mean I was learning to keep my thoughts to myself? Or to take him seriously? Or something else? As I opened my mouth to ask, I could hear the school bus stop down the block. He Who Waits disappeared before I could speak. I gladly headed out the front door and toward the bus stop.

Zach, Maddie and Kenzie all tumbled from the bus amid a torrent of giggles and shouts. I mentally switched gears and was in mom-mode less than twenty seconds later. Afternoon snacks were distributed, school clothes were changed out of and dinner was started within the next half hour.

I was glad to be able to forget about the day's interviews.

The evening continued in much the same way, family-focused and kid-friendly, until around eight o'clock, when Mother called. I hadn't spoken with her since before the accident. Truthfully, I'd been avoiding it.

"Cerridwen, how was your day, dear?" Her Irish lilt seemed extremely annoying this evening.

"Mother, how could you? Do you have any idea how much trouble—"

"Tisk. You'll be fine, lass," Mother interrupted. "You're in a position now to have that agent listen to you."

"Yes, but—"

"But nothing! The Universe needed him to listen to you. The Universe made that happen."

I sighed. "And you decided to help the Universe?"

"Watch your tone, lass." Mother's reprimand reminded me of my teenage years, but her voice softened a bit as she continued. "People are put in your path for a reason. It's okay to ask for their help."

"And some people are thrust into your life by force," I mumbled. Louder, I added, "Well, this guy isn't really asking for my help either, Mother."

"Sometimes we don't know what kind of help we need."

Having had similar conversations with her before, I knew there was no arguing with Mother. "So how can I help you, Ma?"

Her laugh was mildly refreshing. I almost forgot I was so frustrated with her.

"I believe, my dear, that I can help you."

With those nine words, I was back to being frustrated. It must have shown, because Matt looked at me quizzically, while holding up the okay sign. I nodded to him while asking Mother what she meant.

"Only that I think you're missing something. You need some more information if you are to help this spirit cross over."

"Excuse me? What do you mean? This is more your thing. Or Wendy's. Not mine."

I headed to the laundry room, offering a silent prayer of thanks to whoever invented such a convenience. I might as well get something accomplished around the house as Ma lectured me.

"A gift doesn't belong to one person, Cerridwen. A gift should always be shared. In addition, all gifts have the option of selecting their own recipients, coming and going as needed."

I kept silent, waiting for Mother to get to her point.

"You know, dear, when you were a child you helped the spirits pass over all the time."

I rolled my eyes as I measured and poured the liquid laundry soap into the machine. Like people need any help after they die. Wait. That's how I got into this mess, isn't it?

My silence meant nothing to my mother. "Anyway, I have been meditating on your problem and I think I have some information for you."

"Okay, Ma. You lost me." Purposely ignoring her comment about the spirits for now, I quickly wracked my brain trying to remember what Mother and Wendy may have said about meditating on other people's problems. I couldn't come up with anything useful. "Why would you have been meditating on my problem?"

"Because you aren't," came Mother's matter-of-fact reply. "Now, this is what was revealed to me. This young man you need to help is surrounded in a green light. He knows something about money. He followed the rules, but that didn't help him. Now he needs you to help him pass over. You need to assist him with his unfinished business."

"Yeah. Thanks, Ma, but I already got that part." I paused. "But if I'm not communicating with the spirit, how can I help him with some mysterious unfinished business?"

I could hear her tapping a pen or pencil against the table and could almost picture her look of polite annoyance as she tried to keep the exasperation out of her voice. "Cerridwen, have you learned nothing? Think of all I have taught you."

"Ma, I—"

She didn't let me finish. "I have to go now, dear. Your father and I have dinner reservations. My love to all."

The silence coming through the phone told me the conversation was over.

After clicking off the receiver, I headed back into the living room, plopped on the couch, and relayed the conversation to Matt, who was sitting in his recliner reading a book.

"Well, can you remember any time that your mom or sister said anything about contacting new spirits? I mean, do you know how to do that?"

I looked carefully at my husband. "You're serious, aren't you?"

"Of course I'm serious." Matt moved over to the couch. He took my hand before continuing. "Honey, weird things happen to you. Face it. They have as long as I've known you. Remember our first date?"

Matt and I had gone out to dinner at the local Mexican restaurant and saw a romantic-comedy movie afterwards. We obviously had a good time and I even remember feeling nervous as we kissed goodnight, but off the top of my head I couldn't remember anything weird about the evening.

"You made me take a different route home, remember?"

When I remained silent, he continued.

"You kept telling me not to take Dodge Street, even though it was the most direct way to get from the theater to your parent's house. You must have told me to take about three other out-of-the way roads before I figured out where we were," Matt remembered. "The next morning I saw on the news that there was a huge accident on Dodge, remember? Three people died."

I hadn't exactly forgotten any of that, but I certainly didn't dwell on that part of the night, either. "Look, I just had a feeling, ya' know? People have *feelings* all the time. It's called intuition. Besides, you're a scientist. You aren't supposed to believe in any of this stuff."

"Scientifically speaking, energy always exists, right? If our soul is energy, what happens to it when our bodies die? Who's to say there's not spirits and ghosts? And if those exist, isn't it possible they need help once in a while? Cerri, I love you for who you are," Matt continued as he reached over and grabbed my hand. "I love all facets of your personality. I love that part of you that knows about bad car accidents before they happen just as much as I love the part of you that reads bedtime stories to the kids. Do what you need to. You aren't going to freak me out."

Matt leaned over and kissed my cheek.

"I'm going to bed, honey," he said before I could respond to his speech. I watched him walk down the hall to the bedroom.

I picked up a word search puzzle book I'd left on the coffee table and looked at the first word on the list: BEWITCHED. Not wanting witches to end up in my word searches, I glanced at the category. TV SHOWS OF THE '60s was printed boldly across the top of the page.

Damn.

Tossing the word search book on the couch, I leaned my head back and sighed. "This isn't going to be easy, is it?"

"No, *Cuwitku*, it will not," came the now-familiar voice of He Who Waits.

I groaned, shutting my eyes even tighter. "You've got to be kidding me."

"This is no time for joking. I have brought you a visitor."

Not in the mood for visitors, I considered pretending to be asleep, but I knew it was too late for that. Besides, I'm nothing if not curious. I took a deep breath, raised my head and slowly opened my eyes. Standing next to the shaman was a more modern looking spirit.

He Who Waits had found a way to bring Scott Curtis to me.

16

The following morning I was still steaming about my uninvited guests.

Since the visit from He Who Waits lasted less than a minute, and the vision of Scott Curtis even less, I could have easily convinced myself I was asleep. Unfortunately, by now I knew better.

I didn't have time to analyze my feelings, though, since the kids had to get off to school.

The phone rang as Zach, Maddie, and Kenzie bounded out of the house. I raced back into the kitchen for the cordless phone, trying to not to let the kids out of my sight for too long. The bus stop may be visible from the front door, but I never took any chances. I wasn't paranoid, just cautious.

"Yeah," I breathed into the phone. It occurred to me that people don't normally answer the phone that way, but I needed to get back to the front door to watch the kids. From outside, I could hear the sounds of other kids joining my three at the bus stop.

"Mrs. Baker? Is everything alright?"

Great. I answer the phone as rude as can be and it's my favorite FBI agent on the other line. Like we needed any more reason to spread the impoliteness. "Yes, fine. How can I help you Agent Oliver?"

"I'll be picking you up at three fifteen today. We're meeting with a few members of Scott Curtis's dart league, as well as the owner of the bar where they usually play."

"I have to be here when the kids get off the bus," I began. "I can't just run off whenever."

"So you will not be able to join me. Correct?" I'm not sure what a smirk sounds like, but I think I heard one in the agent's voice. "Fine. I'll just—"

"No, I'll be ready. See you then."

I hung up before my mouth had the opportunity to betray me any further.

Aloud I almost shrieked in frustration. "Where did that come from?"

A low chuckle came from behind me. "Open mouth, insert foot?" Matt asked as I spun around.

"You scared the hell out of me! What are you doing home?"

"I forgot some papers I needed. What's going on?"

Quickly, I recapped the conversation with Agent Oliver.

"Not a problem, honey. I'll cut my office hours early today and be home for the kids. Go find the truth with your magic lasso."

I rolled my eyes. "So now I'm Wonder Woman?"

"You are to me," he replied. After a quick peck on the lips, Matt was out the door once again. And he took a great deal of my apprehension with him.

I spent the rest of the day doing mundane household chores and checking my e-mail every few hours. I'd already submitted my Devils Tower article and was expecting to make some revisions. Sarah Martin, the editor of the children's magazine, was usually pretty quick about editing articles and getting them back to the author. I knew Sarah had received my article and the pictures I selected, but I still hadn't heard back about any changes she wanted.

With all that to keep me occupied, the afternoon came much quicker than I expected. At three o'clock, I quickly changed into something more appropriate than the shorts and grungy T-shirt I had been wearing. I just finished dressing when Matt returned home.

"Hate to tell ya' this, but I think I was followed." Matt's eyes darted from side to side as he pretended to whisper in my ear.

My exasperation obviously showed.

"Not funny, huh? Well, your FBI agent is waiting in the driveway."

A quick thanks to Matt for making it home, but not for his warped sense of humor, and I was out the door. The sooner we left, the sooner this experience would be over and I could go back to my normal life.

Agent Oliver was once again quiet during most of the drive from our subdivision to Rapid City. As we neared the city limits, he finally spoke.

"We'll go the Valley Sports Bar first. That's where the dart league meets. Same rules as before. Let me do the talking." The agent punctuated his last statement by glaring at me. Maybe it was my imagination, but the scowl might not have been so icy.

We'd reached the bar. The building could have been mistaken for a small town community center, except I had never seen "Bikers Welcome" or "Monday Night Football" banners sponsored by various beer companies on any community center. I hadn't seen many community centers with steel doors, either.

The bar seemed a little out of the way, but I didn't go to bars that often. By the time I thought to ask the lawman, Agent Oliver was already out of the car and waiting impatiently for me to follow.

Inside the bar, I was expecting to be assaulted with a haze of cigarette smoke and stale body odor. Instead, the aroma of cheeseburgers and fries welcomed us. There wasn't much of a crowd—a few video poker players in the corner and an older man sitting at one of the tables. A too-thin waitress was talking to the burly bartender at the far end of the bar. They both looked up as we walked in, each one sizing us up. No wonder they stared, I couldn't imagine this place had too many suit-and-tie clients on a typical afternoon. But I could be wrong.

Looking around, I could see this was the ultimate sports bar. There were three big screen televisions against one wall, what looked like half a basketball court at the other end of the building, a few pool tables and foosball tables. NFL, NASCAR, MLB, and NBA paraphernalia decorated the walls. The video poker machines seemed out of place.

Agent Oliver stepped up to the bar, introduced himself, and asked to talk to the manager.

The bartender, who looked as if he could bench press me, nodded his head once. "I'm Mac. What can I do for ya'?"

The FBI agent's eyes narrowed. "You're the manager? Is there somewhere a bit more private we can talk?"

"Nora! Watch the bar!" To us he said, "Come with me."

We followed Mac through a door I hadn't noticed when I first came in. By the sounds of things, we were much closer to the kitchen. As he led us into a back office, the light bounced off the bald spot on Mac's head. I couldn't imagine anyone teasing him about his loss of hair, though. I firmly believed he would rather have choked me than be reminded he was going bald.

Inside the office, Mac sat behind the metal desk that looked like it had been bought from a government surplus auction. He leaned forward and the bottom half of a cartoon cat tattoo peeked out from under the sleeve of his worn T-shirt.

Agent Oliver took the padded chair across from the bartender, leaving me with the weak and uncomfortable looking folding chair in the corner.

At the FBI agent's request, Mac introduced himself as Irvin MacIntire. I was sure the only person who had ever called him Irvin was his mother.

As Agent Oliver pulled out a picture of Scott Curtis and explained why we were here, I took in our surroundings. The walls looked as if they'd been painted over more times than they should have. Bits of different colored paint showed through the latest layer of cream. A calendar featuring a half-clothed woman advertising some beer company was tacked to the wall behind the desk. In addition to the desk and three chairs, the office furniture consisted of a filing cabinet and a printer stand. The desk didn't hold anything unusual—a phone, a computer, and a pile of folders were all covering a large desk calendar that looked like it was used for everything from time off requests to special event notices.

Mac's nasally New York accent brought me out of my observations. "I read about him. You really think he was offed?"

Agent Oliver cleared his throat, as if Mac's choice of words disturbed him. "That's one possibility we're investigating."

"I'll be damned." Mac leaned back in his chair and propped his feet on the desk. The tail of the tattooed cat twitched as Mac crossed his arms over his chest. "Never thought he'd have gotten himself whacked."

"Odd choice of words."

The bartender chuckled. "Yeah, well, he was one of the most straight-laced guys I've ever seen in this place. Some of these other guys I could see getting knocked off. This guy? Nope."

Agent Oliver asked Mac to elaborate and the bartender seemed more than willing to comply. Mac didn't say anything surprising about Scott Curtis, though. He was a loner, a bit straight-laced, and totally out of place in the crowded bar.

"I guess I'm trying to say that I really didn't know him, ya' know? These are just my observations."

"And have you had a lot of practice observing people?" The FBI Agent drew the question out as if he had all day for this. I wished he'd hurry it up. My chair was beyond uncomfortable.

Mac's eyes narrowed and I wondered if he was going to throw us out. There was an unmistakable edge to his voice when he spoke. "I've been bouncing and tending bar for over twenty years. I have a degree in sociology from NYU. Yeah, I've had practice." Mac's head seemed to punctuate each sentence with a slight nod.

Agent Oliver stared at the larger man for a moment in some macho attempt to tell if the bartender was lying. I knew he wasn't.

Finally the agent broke the silence. "What else did you observe concerning Mr. Curtis?"

"Not a lot," Mac conceded. "To be honest, he was the least interesting of the guys on his league. Pretty stable. Not a drunk. Good people skills. Good tipper. The waitresses like him well enough. I only ever had but one problem with him, and that wasn't even his fault."

A look of surprise flashed across Agent Oliver's eyes so quickly I would have missed it if I hadn't been looking directly at him.

"Explain," the agent ordered.

Mac sighed. "It was maybe a month or so ago, I guess, on league night. One of the other guys *is* a troublemaker. He usually picks on somebody 'til that person is no longer a challenge. He ain't nothing but a bully and a drunk. A mean drunk at that." A flicker of sadness danced across Mac's face as he spoke.

Mac started to retell the evening in such detail I could picture the whole thing in my mind. I half-expected cheesy "flashback" special effects to accompany the voice-over for my mind's eye.

Mac explained how the bar normally looked when the league showed up. The burger-and-fries atmosphere we noticed earlier was replaced with the stale beer smell I expected. "It's a bar. People drink. People get loud. This night was probably about four, maybe five weeks ago. Scott was here with the rest of the league and their girls. Course, Scott was always alone. The wives and steadies kept trying to fix him up, but it never worked.

"I don't think he was gay or nothing. He was just real picky." Mac shot a quick, almost embarrassed glance in my direction. It was then that I realized Mac had probably turned down many a woman's request for a date. It was not an image I wanted stuck in my head.

"Um, so anyways," Mac continued, "Scott was here and the other guy, Kevin Kirk, he was here. Now Kevin, that's the bully I was tellin' ya' about, he'd been in for a few hours already. And he'd been tossin' back shots."

From the distasteful look on Mac's face, I knew it wasn't unusual for Kevin to be drinking long before the rest of his dart league showed up. Next to me Agent Oliver shifted in his seat.

Mac continued his story. "He and Tina—"

"Tina?" Agent Oliver's eyes seemed to light up at the prospect of another lead.

"Tina Collins is Kevin's girlfriend," Mac replied. "She's as messed up as he is."

"What do you mean?"

"Man, she drinks at least as much as Kevin. He thinks he's God's gift to women, and she thinks she's hot stuff. Really, though, he's an ass and she's nothing to write home about, if you know what I mean."

Agent Oliver nodded, as he made notes in his ever-present notebook.

After a minute, Mac continued. "Anyway, he and Tina had been in here most of the day. And neither one was all that polite by the time the league started."

Mac paused again. It was obviously difficult for him to relate the story, although I wasn't sure why.

"Anyway, Scott got here first, like he usually does, probably about ten or fifteen minutes before the rest of his team, and he's talking with Kevin and Tina."

"Were you able to hear what they were talking about?" Agent Oliver asked.

Mac shook his head. "No, I was too far away. And it wasn't like they were making a scene or anything. At least not then."

"What do you mean?" I asked this question, earning me a glare from the man beside me. So much for keeping my mouth shut. Again.

"It was later that night," Mac said. "Tina actually poured her drink on Scott. I don't know why or what led up to that, but afterwards, we had to escort all three of them out of the bar."

Agent Oliver beat me to the next question. "And you don't know why she poured her drink on him? You didn't hear anything?"

Mac shifted in his chair. "I didn't say that. Look, I didn't mean to, but I did hear part of the argument. Or at least what I think led up to the argument. See, Tina was hitting on Scott pretty hard. She had been for a few weeks. And Scott wasn't taking the bait."

As Mac continued to relay his version of the evening, his story-telling abilities began to shine once again. I could almost picture myself in the bar watching the events unfold.

The bartender finished relaying how Kevin accused Scott of hitting on Tina and how the three were asked to leave. He went on to say that Kevin and Tina had to be forcibly removed, while Scott was more compliant.

"And that's all I know, seriously. Tina was screaming that it was actually Scott hitting on her and Kevin was yelling about how Scott needed to keep his hands to himself, and Scott was real quiet-like. Super calm. I wouldn't have handled those two as well."

"Do you know where we can find Tina or Kevin?" asked Agent Oliver.

Mac gave the lawman what information he had and we stood to leave.

Agent Oliver pulled a *Columbo*-style move as we headed out the door. "Just one more thing."

Inwardly, I groaned. Maybe he wasn't a jerk. Maybe he was nothing more than a bad stereotype.

"Where were you the night Scott was killed?"

Mac's eyes narrowed for a split second, once again insinuating that he usually demanded answers, not the other way around. "I was here. Doing inventory. No, nobody kept track of me."

"Really. Interesting."

"What I can do, though, is give you a copy of the inventory sheets. Can't prove when I did it, but at least it was done." The edge hadn't left Mac's voice and I was hoping I wouldn't be witness to some juvenile show of machismo.

Much to my surprise, Agent Oliver turned and left.

Even more surprising, He Who Waits appeared. "Follow him. He needs your guidance."

I hustled after Agent Oliver.

17

I didn't actually catch up to Agent Oliver until he was in the car. By then, he had the key in the ignition and was slamming shut his cell phone. I barely had time to get in the vehicle before he slammed the gearshift from park to reverse. The scowl on his face was even more pronounced.

"Wow. I didn't think it was possible."

"What?" came Agent Oliver's grunt. My words had caused him to stop what he was doing. He didn't start pulling out of the bar's parking lot like I thought he would, instead he just stared at me.

"Um . . . I didn't think you could actually be any ruder, if you want to know the truth." All the smart-aleck comments running through my head no longer seemed so clever when they could easily be said aloud to an upset federal agent.

Agent Oliver glared at me.

As long as I had started, I might as well continue. No matter how much I wished it might, the earth didn't seem ready to open up and swallow me whole for telling off Special Agent Jerk. It actually felt nice to get some of my frustration off my chest. "Look, your people skills are lousy. There was no need to be an ass in there."

No surprise, but Agent Oliver kept glaring. Thankfully, his cell phone rang.

"Oliver . . . Right . . . Kevin Kirk." He grabbed the notebook and pen from his jacket pocket. "The root beer plant off the interstate . . . Right . . . Driver, okay. And Tina Collins?" Another pause. "Family Thrift Center cashier. Which store? East side? . . . Okay, we're headed there next. Thanks, Susan." He flipped his phone shut.

There was an uncomfortable silence as we drove the few blocks to the nearest grocery store.

Agent Oliver broke the silence as he pulled into the parking lot. "Susan, the office secretary, says Tina works here. Let's get her version."

Neither of us spoke again until we were inside the store. Family Thrift Center was a mid-priced grocery store. Nothing fancy, but people could find most of what they were looking for stocked on the shelves. There were three in town, one on the west side, one on the east side and one pretty much in the middle. According to local stereotypes, everything on the west side of Rapid City catered to a wealthier crowd, including grocery stores. The east-side store didn't have the same frills as the other two, but it wasn't a dive, either.

Once in the store, Agent Oliver did his "power" thing. The manager, a short, dumpy fellow who probably started out as a bag boy and one day found himself shocked to be running the place, had a look of terror on his face from the moment Agent Oliver flicked his credentials. Oddly, though, this time the FBI agent introduced me, as well. Not that it changed the manager's expression any.

The manager gave us all the pertinent information about Tina Collins—address, phone number, age, how long she'd worked at the store, what kind of employee she was. I'm sure he would have handed her personnel file over to Agent Oliver directly if he had asked for it.

Tina's employment record wasn't extraordinary. She had never been employee of the month, but she didn't have a stack of reprimands, either. I noticed that Agent Oliver read the information, but took very few notes.

The FBI agent and I were left alone in the manager's office while he went to get Tina, who, it turned out, was working.

"What do you think?" The gruffness of Agent Oliver's tone was milder and he sounded almost compassionate.

For a moment I wasn't sure who he was speaking to. By the time I realized Agent Oliver was actually speaking to me, the manager returned with a woman I could only assume was Tina. She was wearing the typical Family Thrift Center cashier uniform of black pants and a dark polo-style shirt. I guessed her height to be around five-foot four and was about twenty pounds too thin. She looked like she was in her late forties, but she was probably ten years younger. She had long, straw-colored hair and light brown eyes. Her skin reminded me of my mother's favorite gloves—dried and leathery, yet well worn. She was smacking gum and her face itself resembled a pug dog's. She didn't look like a nice person, and I immediately distrusted her.

As I studied Tina's appearance, I tried to remember everything I could about the woman I knew killed Scott Curtis. Was Tina the right height? Tina's hair seemed a little too dark. She did, however, seem to be vicious enough to commit such a heinous crime.

At least those were my first impressions.

Back in "jerk-mode" Agent Oliver sprang on Tina the moment she entered the room.

"Tina Collins. Have a seat." There was no compassion in his voice now. "How well did you know Scott Curtis?"

"Um, I didn't. Well, not really." Tina's eyes darted around the room and beads of sweat appeared on her upper lip. She was obviously lying and I was sure Agent Oliver didn't need me to point it out.

Agent Oliver remained silent for what seemed like an eternity before he finally said, "Explain."

Tina rehashed much of what Mac had said about the dart league and Scott's involvement there without adding new details. I noticed she avoided any mention of a fight between Scott and her boyfriend, Kevin. When she finished her monologue, Agent Oliver again allowed the silence to build, making Tina visibly nervous.

"How did you and Scott get along?" Agent Oliver's voice held no emotion as he asked the question and it occurred to me that interviewing someone for a police investigation was a lot like interviewing someone for an article—sometimes you had to ask questions you already knew the answer to because you needed to hear the other person say something in particular. In this case, I was pretty sure Agent Oliver wanted to hear how Tina would describe her relationship with the dead man.

Tina's eyes narrowed ever-so-slightly. I imagined she was trying to decide exactly how to answer his question. "He was a jackass, okay. I didn't like him."

As soon as the words were out of her mouth, I wanted to start laughing. She reminded me of the twins denying their culpability when I asked if one had hit the other, right after I watched the entire assault happen.

"Really? So you didn't like him at all?" came Agent Oliver's retort.

"No, I didn't. He was a snob. He acted like he was all better than everybody cuz he had a college degree or something." Tina's voice had started to take on a vulgar quality that reminded me more of the bar than anything Mac had said earlier. I may have imagined it, but I could have sworn her head flipped from side to side as she continued her tirade. "Frankly, he treated everyone like crap because they weren't all perfect like him."

This was the real Tina Collins: rough, gruff, and more than slightly obnoxious. My mother had a phrase for women like her, and it wasn't very nice.

"And how, exactly, did he treat you?" Tina's true colors didn't seem to faze Agent Oliver. I silently hoped I'd never become so jaded.

Tina leaned farther back in her chair, adopting one of the most defiant poses I'd seen outside of a *Law & Order* episode. "Scott was always using big words to show how smart he was. That was when he bothered to talk to us peons in the first place. Most of the time he couldn't lower himself to talk to us peasants."

"Peasants," repeated Agent Oliver skeptically.

"Um, yeah." I could almost hear the word "duh" in Tina's reply. "I'm telling you he was a jackass. Frankly, I was surprised he even bothered to grace us with his presence."

"So you wouldn't have tried to hit on him on anything, right?" The tone Agent Oliver used implied that he'd dealt with women of fickle affections like this one more than once. I wondered briefly about his home life before Tina's vehement denial brought me back to the present.

"Good gawd, no! Haven't you been listening at all?" She rolled her eyes as she turned her body more toward me. "Is he always this thick? Besides, me and Kevin, we are so going to get married!"

Tina looked at me like I was some sort of confidant, so I decided to take her lead.

"Really? Have you set a date yet?" I was trying my best to sound interested. In reality, I didn't care and wasn't sure why I even asked her the question.

Tina ran her hand quickly through her thin hair, pausing to twirl her ponytail for a minute before replying. "Well, no. Not yet. We're waiting until Kevin gets the raise he was promised. Ya' know, it takes a lot to bring up a family these days, and between us, we have three kids already. Plus the rent and that little thing with his soon-to-be-ex-wife . . ."

Gee, this one's a real winner. "Yeah, child support and alimony can be rough," I said.

"Oh, it ain't that. I have a fine I need to pay from when I tried to run her ass over."

That left me speechless. Tina must have mistook my silence as interest, because she kept going. "I mean, it's not like I actually hurt her or anything. And if she hadn't been trying to get Kevin back, it wouldn't have happened anyway. Stupid b—"

I'd forgotten the manager was still hanging around until he coughed, ever so slightly. I couldn't be sure, though, if he was trying to keep Tina from cursing, or if he was trying to protect her from saying too much.

Agent Oliver shot the manager a look of dismissal before taking the opportunity to reclaim control of the questioning. The manager didn't get the hint and stayed put. "Was this recently?"

Tina shrugged. "Six months ago, I guess. I know I got hauled off to jail and almost lost my job because of her."

I glanced at the manager, who nodded his agreement; his beet-red face a testimony to his obvious discomfort.

Agent Oliver seemed oblivious. "What exactly were you charged with?"

It was only logical that law enforcement officer would get all the details later, so I assumed he was asking to see how truthful Tina would be.

"Assault with a deadly weapon," spat the woman. She turned to face me. "Can you believe that crock?"

Agent Oliver slammed shut his notebook and put it back in the breast pocket of his suit jacket. "I think that's all for now, Miss Collins. We will be in touch."

As shocked as I was at Tina's cavalier attitude about past events, and as positive as I was that she was capable of murder, I didn't think she had done it. Scott's murder seemed well thought out and Tina didn't strike me as a thinker.

Now I just had to figure out a way to tell that to Agent Oliver.

18

I was still in a state of shock and Tina's revelation, when we got to the car. Her caviler attitude over what had to be attempted murder left me flabbergasted.

"Weren't expecting that one, were you?"

Gee, that was an understatement. Of course I wasn't prepared for my companion's change in attitude, either. Aloud I said simply, "No. Did you know she had tried to run someone over?"

With a shrug, Agent Oliver started the car and we were off again. This time he headed toward a more industrial part of Rapid City. I glanced at my watch, wondering if we would hit the five o'clock rush.

"Relax. Shouldn't be too much longer."

For a moment, I didn't realize Agent Oliver had been the one speaking. Like the flick of a switch, his tone had softened. I was almost too stunned to reply. If his kindness continued, I was afraid I'd have to change my opinion of him, and I *really* didn't want to do that. Immediately after having that thought I heard the deep chuckle of He Who Waits reverberate through my mind.

Clearly, He Who Waits and I would be discussing this later.

Having been lost in my own thoughts, I didn't realize we had arrived at the root beer plant. Kevin Kirk was easy for me to pick out among the people scattered throughout the parking lot—he was the one who looked the most upset and inconvenienced. Of course, it helped that He Who Waits was standing next to him.

Since I didn't share any of that with Agent Oliver, he went the traditional route and asked someone to point out our next interview.

Leaning against a beat-up, older-model, tan pick-up truck, Kevin Kirk displayed an air of being both bored and aggravated at the same time. His shaggy blond hair, covered by a dirty baseball cap, was kept out of his eyes only by his aviator style prescription lenses. Kevin's bulky arms were crossed in front of his generous belly. At least thirty pounds overweight, I assumed Kevin avoided regular exercise.

"Looks can be deceiving, *Cuwitku*." The voice of He Who Waits broke into my thoughts once again. I debated replying, but decided I didn't need to look like I was talking to myself.

We parked next to the pickup and got out of the car without

Agent Oliver giving me another speech about keeping silent while he conducted his interview. I wasn't sure if his lack of lecture meant he trusted me to ask intelligent questions, or if he had decided I would probably ask something no matter what. Either way, I was grateful to skip that part.

As I stepped out of the car, I felt a rush of wind and heard the *splat* of something hitting the pavement. I looked down and felt the overwhelming urge to gag at the amount of chew that had barely missed my shoe.

Kevin nodded. "Sorry 'bout that. Should watch where you're going."

"Or you could try not to spit that crap out around a lady," came Agent Oliver's quick retort. "You Kevin Kirk?"

"You must be the fed who wanted to meet me. Whatcha want?" Kevin's voice had a vague Southern accent.

"We just want to ask you a few questions," said Agent Oliver, while pretending to look around the parking lot. I noticed he never really let Kevin out of his sight, or turned his back on him though. "Is there somewhere a little more private? Or we could head back to my office and talk there."

"There's a break room here we can use." Kevin led the way through the plant's employee entrance.

Once in the break room, Agent Oliver pulled out a tape recorder and made the introductions and explained why we were there. I rummaged through my pocket for some change and bought a pop from the vending machine in the corner before sitting at the table where the men where.

"I don't see what I can tell you. It's not like Scott and I were buddies or anything."

"You did socialize, though, didn't you?"

Kevin's face took on a blank look for a moment before he replied. "You mean the dart league? I wouldn't call that socializin.'"

The two men continued their conversation, Agent Oliver asking the same questions he'd covered with the others we'd talked to and Kevin giving more or less the same old answers. Listening to the dialogue, it was all I could do to keep my mind from wandering. I was sore and tired and wanted to be back at home vegging in front of the television.

Plus, I knew Kevin didn't kill Scott. A woman had. I hadn't totally ruled out Tina Collins, but Kevin Kirk was in the clear for this crime.

What a waste of time.

I stole a glance at my watch, trying to be sly about it. Instead, I managed to knock over the pop can.

A string of expletives left Kevin's mouth as the sticky, carbonated beverage covered the table. "Damn it! You know who has to clean up that crap, dontcha?"

Agent Oliver growled something under his breath. I wasn't sure if the growl was directed at Kevin or at me and I wasn't going to ask. To be honest, I was afraid to.

Once the mess had been sopped up, Agent Oliver steered the conversation back to Kevin's relationship with Scott. "How often did you see Scott? You were both regulars with the dart league. How did you two get along?"

Kevin's lip curled as he glared at the agent. "Didn't do your research, did ya'? I didn't like the guy. I only saw him at the bar. He wasn't worth my time."

I couldn't tell for sure if Kevin really only saw Scott at the bar, or if Kevin believed that Scott wasn't worth his time. Either way, my internal lie-detector was pinging off the charts. I tossed a glance in Agent Oliver's direction, but I couldn't be sure he was picking up the same vibes I was.

"Really?" began Agent Oliver. "Not worth your time? Then what was the argument about?"

The way Kevin's jaw dropped could have inspired a Saturday morning cartoon. I resisted the urge to giggle.

"Well . . . um . . . see . . . um . . ."

"Look, Kevin. Why don't you just cut to the chase? You had an argument with Scott Curtis. You have a history of violence. You threatened him. Less than a month later, he was dead." Agent Oliver paused, scowling at the man sitting across the table. "So why don't you cut the crap and tell us what really happened?"

Kevin was silent for a few minutes and I watched his eyes glide left and right. He was either trying to remember what happened, or trying to remember what lie he had already told about it. Either way, I didn't think we'd be getting anything close to the truth at this point.

"Look, man, I didn't like the guy. We'd had words. He was a horse's ass, but I didn't kill him." Kevin leaned back a little in his chair and crossed his arms over his chest. I had the distinct impression Kevin was convinced the action made him look tough and powerful. He actually looked like a spoiled little kid.

My mothering instinct made watch Kevin closely. I'd had to deal with too many temper tantrums when the kids were toddlers to not recognize one coming. Maybe it was because I was watching him so intently, but I noticed the change that had occurred in his eyes. While his actions made him look like a brat, there was a hardness in his eyes that reminded me more of a thug. I liked Kevin even less.

While all this was racing around in my head, Agent Oliver continued the interview, his tone matching Kevin's defiant posture.

"What did you argue with him about?"

"I dunno. Dumb shit, I guess. Can't remember."

"Really." Agent Oliver didn't sound convinced. He didn't really look convinced either. I was pretty sure I was going to be in the middle of yet another macho stare down. Didn't men ever just call someone on a lie? Or was it that FBI agents didn't? Either way, this macho thing was getting really old.

The two men kept babbling—Agent Oliver asking questions and Kevin giving short, evasive answers—for another twenty minutes or so. Meanwhile, I was bored to death. For once I actually wished I could make He Who Waits show up, just so I'd have something else to focus on. This interview was getting us nowhere.

I was starting to wonder again why I had to be here when Agent Oliver's now-familiar conclusion tone broke into my thoughts.

I grabbed my purse and was starting to stand up, grateful to be done with the boredom. I was tired and sore and frustrated. And that's when He Who Waits actually did decide to make an appearance.

"You couldn't have shown up a half hour ago and saved me from some of this boredom?" I wanted to scream, but thought better of it. It was bad enough that he had to show up when I was finally getting to leave here, I didn't need the two men in the room to think I'd totally lost it. For a split second I contemplated not acknowledging He Who Waits at all. Recent experience suggested that plan probably wouldn't work out so well, either.

"He knows more than he says," stated He Who Waits, nodding toward Kevin.

I thought my head might explode. If He Who Waits knew who the murderer was, why not just tell Agent Oliver or somebody else and be done with it? Instead of verbalizing any of that, though, I just rolled my eyes. Again.

"This man is not the only one who has argued with Scott. Find out who else did." With those cryptic words, He Who Waits vanished before my eyes.

I must have gasped or sighed or something because I noticed Agent Oliver staring at me. "Did you have something to add?" he asked.

Looking at Kevin I asked, "Did Scott have a problem with anyone else?"

"How would I know?" Kevin glared at me, but in a flash his face softened just a bit and he sat up a little straighter, even leaning toward me some. "Wait a sec! He did have a beef with someone."

He Who Waits's head appeared and nodded before fading back into the wall, reminding me of the Cheshire cat.

Agent Oliver stopped and stared first at Kevin, then at me.

I waited for Kevin to continue. When he didn't, I pushed the issue. "Who? Do you know what it was about?"

He shook his head. "Nope. I just heard him getting into it with someone on the phone."

The FBI agent resumed the interrogation. "What did you hear? And when?"

Kevin rubbed the back of his neck. He seemed to visibly relax once he realized this revelation threw at least some suspicion off of him. "He was on his cell phone talking to his old lady. Sounded like she was ripping him a new one, too."

"His old lady?" I asked. "Scott wasn't married."

"Sure sounded like his old lady," came the reply. "She was gripping about something and he was all 'Yes,' 'Okay,' 'I understand.' Trying to be sweet or something. Held up the dart match that night for a good ten or fifteen minutes."

"When was that?" asked Agent Oliver.

Kevin thought for a moment. "I dunno. A month or so ago, I guess."

I was disappointed. I sort of hoped that Kevin would blurt out "Oh, with some woman Jane and she threatened to shoot him. Would you like her address and phone number? I have that information, too." My face must have given me away.

Kevin looked at me and added, "Hey, I didn't think it meant anything. I mean, he was quiet. Never volunteered information. I sorta wondered if maybe his old lady wasn't beatin' the crap outta him. Would have explained a lot."

"What do you mean?" I asked.

"A guy ain't normally that quiet. Not a real man, that is."

Kevin's arrogance was finally getting on my last nerve. "Why would you assume the phone call had anything to do with a woman?"

"Cuz I know what it's like when my old lady is reading me the riot act. Can't get a word in edgewise." Kevin shrugged. "That's how he was actin'."

"And which 'old lady' would that be?" asked Agent Oliver.

"Your wife? Or your girlfriend?"

Although I hadn't thought it possible, Kevin became even more smug. I wondered if he was that stupid for being an ass to a federal agent or if he was really that full of himself. I decided I would have to ask Matt about the inner workings of a man's mind when I got home.

And men say women are difficult to understand.

Kevin answered with yet another shrug. "Divorces are expensive," was his only answer.

Agent Oliver shook his head slightly, as if to say "Is this guy serious?"

"You won't get divorced because it's expensive, so you have a girlfriend on the side? Are you serious? And everybody's okay with that? Is your wife an idiot, too?" Well, that's what I really wanted to say. Instead I snorted. Not very lady-like, but I really couldn't help myself.

Yet another flash of anger passed across Kevin's face and I was grateful when Agent Oliver once again took control. "So you think Scott was getting the third degree from his wife or girlfriend. Know anything about her?"

Kevin shook his head. "Nope."

"All right, I think that's all for now." The FBI agent reached for his cassette recorder. "If you think of anything, let me know. And we will be in touch."

Agent Oliver rose, handed Kevin a business card, and led the way out of the break room. I thought I heard the sound of paper ripping and glanced over my shoulder to see Kevin ripping the card in two.

Kevin noticed and, using his thumb and index finger in the shape of a gun, made a shooting motion before grinning like an evil villain from the movies.

I hurriedly ran after Agent Oliver. I wanted to get as far away from Kevin Kirk as possible.

19

By the time we got out of the building and back in the car, I was once again regretting that anonymous phone call to the tip line. Investigating a death—let alone a murder—wasn't what I wanted to do with my life anyway. I was a mom and a wife and a sometimes writer. Not an investigator.

Come to think of it, I didn't want anything to do with the police, either. I preferred my mysteries in book form.

"All right, I guess we can call it a day." Agent Oliver interrupted my thoughts.

I breathed a sigh of relief. "Finally!" I honestly hadn't meant to say that aloud. Sometimes I speak first, and think later.

In the driver's seat, Agent Oliver started to chuckle.

"You think it's funny? I mean, I'm probably too overjoyed to be done, but I don't think this is funny." I sounded indigent, even to my own ears. "In fact, that guy gave me the creeps." I opted to leave out Kevin's parting gesture, especially since I knew he wasn't the murderer we were after.

"Hey, I didn't mean anything by it. Honest," started the agent as he pulled back onto the main road.

For a moment, he sounded almost friendly. Almost. The next time he spoke, Agent Oliver's voice had resumed its professional undertone. "So, what did you pick up? Anything?"

"Not much," I said. "Kevin's not a very nice person, that's for sure. But he didn't kill Scott." He Who Waits had told me it was a woman who killed Scott Curtis, but I wasn't sure how to share that bit of information with the disbelieving man sitting next to me. All our past experience taught me that Agent Oliver wouldn't believe me, so I tried to come up with some compelling reason why I believed Kevin wasn't the guy.

Agent Oliver nodded. "I think you're right."

I almost missed his agreement. "Excuse me? What did you say?"

"I said I think you're right. I agree with you. Kevin's a dirt bag, but he didn't do this."

Agent Oliver thought I was right? My entire world had just turned upside-down. What had changed his opinion of me?

"Oh." I didn't know what to say, but felt I needed to respond in some way. I couldn't just blurt out that a spirit had told me the killer was a woman, but I certainly wasn't prepared for Agent Oliver to agree with me, either. "So, um, any idea who the woman was? The woman Kevin mentioned?"

"No, unfortunately. We haven't been able to find anything about a woman in a relationship with Scott."

As long as Agent Oliver was being civil, this seemed like a good time to go out on a limb and try to accomplish the absurd mission I'd been given. "Do you think a woman could have killed him?"

That was a ridiculous question. Of course, he thought a woman could have killed Scott. He thought I had killed Scott. As stupid as the question sounded to me, it didn't seem to bother Agent Oliver. Or else he opted to ignore the irony of it.

I did hope it planted a seed that would send him in the right direction, though.

"Yes, I do. There were some footprints at Devils Tower that we believe belonged to the murderer. They were smaller, like a woman's print." Agent Oliver's voice filled the car. "Besides, guns are unisex."

"I thought women didn't usually kill with a gun."

"Just because they don't doesn't mean they can't." His voice had taken on a resigned tone, as if the violence he tried to correct in his career had started to jade other parts of his life as well.

I didn't know how to reply. The combination of shock that he seemly trusted me combined with the heavy tone our conversation had taken left me dumbfounded.

By the time we arrived at the Federal Building, I was over my shock but still didn't know what to do next. I hoped we'd be done and I could forget all about my short brush with law enforcement. It would make a great story to retell in the future—very far in the future that is. I got out of the FBI sedan and began walking to my own car.

"Ten a.m. tomorrow," came the deep voice of Agent Oliver.

I turned around, almost twisting my ankle in the process. It felt like something, or someone, held my foot in place. I was sure I knew where to place the blame, but how do you punish an ancient spirit?

Once my foot was freed I quickly took a small step forward, trying to make it look as if I'd stumbled on a rock. Unfortunately, I took the charade too far and started to really fall. I felt a pair of strong arms around me, steadying me and keeping me from landing on my face. Embarrassed, I looked up to see the face of my rescuer. There was no one I could see, but the scent of leather permeated my nostrils. Obviously, He Who Waits had kept me from landing on my face. I'd have to thank him next time he decided to show himself.

"What the hell just happened?" Agent Oliver's voice had taken a tone somewhere between awed and frightened.

"I, um, must have tripped. My leg is still bothering me from the car accident." I hoped that sounded plausible even if I was rambling.

The look on Agent Oliver's face told me he wasn't fooled at all.

"You didn't trip," began the FBI agent. "You did, but you didn't. You tripped. And should have fallen. But you didn't. Why?" Agent Oliver was repeating himself, almost stumbling over his words. Obviously, my phantom rescuer had rattled the usually rational man.

"Don't know. Luck, I guess." The answer sounded lame, even to me.

Out of the corner of my eye, He Who Waits materialized for a moment, shook his head once, and disappeared again. The visitation happened so quickly I was sure I had imagined it.

Except now I didn't know if He Who Waits was trying to tell me not to continue with my lie about being lucky, or if he was saying not to tell the truth about what just happened. My mother's words came back to me: "The spirits are funny creatures." Just what I needed—to be reminded of the uncertainty of spirits I'd rather left me alone anyway.

"That wasn't luck," began Agent Oliver, "it was something else." He didn't say another word as he turned and headed into the Federal Building.

I managed to make it all the way back to my car without another incident. Good thing, since I was seething. In the less than thirty paces from where I'd mysteriously tripped to the safety of my car, I managed to turn my embarrassment into righteous indignation. As soon as the car door slammed shut, I began my verbal assault on the spirit world.

"What was that about? You freakin' pushed me!" I was conscious of the fact I was alone in the car. Some woman in a well-tailored business suit glared at me as if she was wondering who the heck I was yelling at. I gave her a "mind your own business" glare, started the car, and backed out of the parking space.

A deep chuckle came from the direction of the backseat at the same time that the smell of leather hit my nostrils.

"There's nothing funny about this," I said through gritted teeth.

"Ah, *Cuwitku*, there is humor in this, as there is in all situations," began He Who Waits. "You need only to look for it."

"Well, I'm so glad I could be your source of humor." I was vaguely aware that I sounded like a spoiled brat. I just didn't care.

"Were you injured?"

"No, but I could have been," I snapped.

"Do you believe I would have allowed that?" The shaman sounded simultaneously disappointed and hurt.

I had to admit that I didn't. "But you still didn't have to push me, did you?"

"Everything is done for a reason, *Cuwitku.* Just because you do not understand at this time, does not mean there is no reason." The rebuke hit home.

We spent the next ten minutes in silence as I pondered his words. I was glad there wasn't a lot of traffic on Highway 79 as I headed for home. The smell of worn leather lingered and I could tell He Who Waits hadn't left.

As we neared my subdivision, I finally broke the uneasy silence. "So what was the point of that? Why push me or trip me or whatever?"

"Because the *wawanyake* needed to see. He is *woawacinhecetu.* He must see to believe."

"What?" These were words I wasn't completely familiar with.

The shaman's brow creased as he tried to translate the words.

"The police needed to see. Your Agent Oliver is a skeptic."

I had reached the intersection just a few blocks from the house and wanted to finish this conversation before reaching the driveway. I certainly didn't want Zach or the girls to see me talking to my "imaginary friend." That would open up questions I didn't want to answer.

Since there wasn't anyone else on the road, I stayed sitting at the stop sign.

"Agent Oliver needed to see? See what? Me fall on my face?" I noticed my voice had lost most of the whinny quality it held before. At least I was starting to accept what was happening in my life, even if I didn't like it.

I rubbed my head, trying to ward off the headache I could feel coming. When I looked back up, He Who Waits had materialized in the front passenger's seat.

"What he saw was not you falling. He saw you being held up."

"He what?"

"The *wawanyake*, your Agent Oliver, saw you being held up. He distinctly saw you not fall."

I pondered that for a moment. "And that is important?"

"Yes. Your Agent Oliver saw something that is not easy explained away, though he will try."

I rubbed my temples again. "I still don't get it."

"You will soon understand."

A horn blared, scaring me but reminding me where I was. I glanced in the rear-view mirror as an impatient driver laid on the horn again. I drove through the intersection. Looking over at the passenger's seat, I saw He Who Waits had vanished.

A feeling of dread had taken his place.

20

The rest of the night passed blissfully uneventful. Well, uneventful on the crime-fighting scene anyway. Kenzie and Maddie decided to gang up on Zach, causing lots of giggles from the girls, a ton of screaming in protest from their brother, and one broken vase when one of Zach's toys missed hitting his sisters. The diversion was just what I needed to put the day's events behind me.

The break from the day's events truly wasn't long enough.

The kids had finally settled down and gone to bed, and Matt was snoring in the living room. I limped to my office to find something to do. Even though I was yawning, I knew I wouldn't get any sleep. My mind wouldn't stay focused and kept leaping between the day's interviews, how to get out of the mess I seemed to be in, and the pain coursing through my leg. I briefly toyed with the idea of taking one of the pain pills I received from the hospital, but I'd never been a big fan of aspirin so taking the prescription-strength medication to help me relax didn't sound appealing, either.

Looking around my office, I decided to organize the room. It was the last area that needed to be unpacked and since I couldn't sleep I decided to be productive.

Once in the room, I sat in the executive-style chair at the desk. The desktop computer, an older Power Mac G4, was already on. Easily distracted, I decided to check my e-mail. Most of the messages were encouraging me to buy a product guaranteed to please my mate or spend hundreds of dollars finding out how to work from home. Just about the time I was wishing Macs came with built-in solitaire, my sister sent me an e-mail.

GET ON YAHOO was all the message stated.

I opened the messenger program and immediately got dinged by Wendy.

I think my house is haunted. What do you think? Wendy typed.

Psychic abilities supposedly come in six different forms, mirroring the five senses plus the mind. When we were little kids, Wendy and I used to pretend we had some of these powers. My sister hasn't stopped pretending. Wendy was much better at clairsentience, or feeling and touching something to get a premonition from. I just knew things—also called claircognizance—and could occasionally hear things, known as clairaudience. We both had some clairvoyant experiences where we thought we saw things. Of course, I've always had an overactive imagination. Very rarely did either of us claim to smell spirits, also called clairalience, and even less often did clairgustance, or tasting, come into our fantasy world.

At least until recently it seemed.

Frustrated that Wendy would continue with the game when we were both in our thirties, I opted to pull rank as "big sister."

Yeah, right, I typed. Houses aren't haunted. Ghosts don't exist.

The words mocked me as the smell of leather briefly filled my nostrils.

I'm serious. Something is messing with my DVD collection.

Grateful that she couldn't see me, I rolled my eyes and started laughing as I pictured a bunch of transparent beings sitting around her living room with a bowl of popcorn watching *Ghostbusters* for horror night. I must have waited too long to respond, because Wendy sent another message.

CERRI . . . You still there? Can you tell if my house is haunted?

Why do you think something is messing with your DVDs?

Because, this morning I found a bunch of DVD cases in the middle of the hallway. My DVDs aren't even stored in the hall!

Barely trying to stop another involuntary eye roll, I decided to humor my sister.

Really? Which DVDs?

That's the weird thing. The movies were Twilight Zone, E.T., *and* Close Encounters.

Are you sure Molly didn't do it?

Molly was a twenty-pound, long-haired, white Persian cat with a nasty disposition and a perpetual eye infection that added nothing positive to her appearance or attitude. Zach had once said that Molly Cat never had to worry about chasing mice because all the mice were too scared to even look at her.

Yeah, a cat can pull three DVDs out from different shelves in the living room and put them all together in the hallway.

Even without the benefit of hearing her voice, Wendy's sarcasm wasn't lost on me.

Before I could type a response, Wendy continued.

Seriously, there's no way Molly could have drug those movies out. Not possible.

So your house is haunted by a Spielberg fan. Yeah, that makes a lot of sense.

I didn't say it made sense!

There was a pause and I could imagine Wendy reaching up to crack her neck, trying to calm herself physically before she completely lost her temper. Finally, she continued.

Don't tell me what you think. Tell me what you feel!

I dunno, Wen. This isn't really my thing, ya know?

As I sent the message, the smell of leather once again filled my nostrils both mocking me and announcing the presence of He Who Waits.

"Your impressions will not fail you. Be true to them and they will be true to you," said He Who Waits from behind me. "Your *tankaku* knows this as well as I."

I fought the urge to argue with the shaman about what my sister knew. I was starting to learn that it didn't accomplish anything.

Suddenly I was tired. *Bone tired* was how Matt would have described it. No longer was I interested in chatting with Wendy. In fact, I wasn't sure I could stifle a yawn if my life depended on it.

Would you at least try to help?

Wendy hadn't seemed to notice my lack of response.

Yeah, yeah. I'll think about it and see if anything comes to me.

I shut the computer down, consoling myself with the fact Wendy never bothered with polite good-byes. I knew it was childish, but I didn't care. I just wanted to crawl into bed and sleep. A deep uninterrupted sleep.

I managed to make it to bed. I even fell asleep for a little while. But it wasn't the restful slumber I had hoped for.

I dreamed of the dart league members I'd met. Only instead of throwing darts they were throwing tarot cards, which stuck to the regulation-style board. He Who Waits was there, cheering on the team. Scott was there, bringing beers to the players. On every table sat a Spielberg movie and the mashed potato sculpture from *Close Encounters of the Third Kind* sat atop a pool table in the back of the room.

I woke up less than refreshed with the odd images still floating around in my head.

21

As I got the kids ready for school, I managed to push the dream to the back of my mind. The more pressing concerns of school clothes and breakfasts and packing lunches and catching the bus took priority. Once the bus pulled away, however, my thoughts went back to the odd dream.

On a rational level, the dream made perfect sense. I'd spent a good chunk of yesterday afternoon interviewing people with Agent Oliver. Tarot cards sticking to a dartboard, though, gave me something to think about.

Knowing myself as I did, I knew the images would stay with me no matter how badly I wanted to forget them. I poured myself a cup of coffee and sat at the kitchen table with a pad of paper and a pen. I began to write everything I could remember about the dream. I got to the point where the dart team was throwing tarot cards and froze. Tarot cards stuck to a dartboard didn't make sense—not even in a dream world. The message had to be the cards themselves. I struggled to remember which cards were thrown. Justice. The Tower. Nine of Swords. Queen of Pentacles. Those were the only ones I remembered.

Justice. That made sense. He Who Waits claimed I was supposed to get justice for the victim. No one could deny Scott needed— deserved—justice for his murder. No surprise in that card.

The Tower. Another card that didn't surprise me at all. The tower meant a total, drastic change. That was certainly true in Scott's life. Or rather, his death. It occurred to me that by even following this line of reasoning—and I used the term loosely—my own life had taken a drastic U-turn. Interesting.

Nine of Swords. The tarot's true death card. Since Scott was clearly murdered, this wasn't a surprise card either.

That left the Queen of Pentacles. I sighed. Court cards were never my favorites. They could mean so many things. This one, I was sure, represented the murderer. If I just could determine who that was I could put this nonsense behind me. For a moment I had a new respect for anyone who chose to spend their time figuring out these life and death puzzles. I hated it.

As I was pondering what made anyone select a career in crime fighting, the doorbell rang. Once again Agent Oliver was standing on my doorstep. Once again I wasn't too happy to see him.

I sighed as I opened the door. "Don't I get a day off?" I knew my voice sounded snippy, but I wasn't in the mood to talk to him. I had too much to think about and Agent Oliver's skepticism was too close to my own. None of this made sense to me, so how was my insight supposed to help find a murderer?

Crossing the threshold, Agent Oliver pulled an over-stuffed manila folder out of a leather pouch. "I brought the case file. Let's talk."

As bossy as that sounded, I detected a note of respect in the FBI agent's words. It shocked me, considering how he spoke to me just a few days ago.

I led Agent Oliver to the kitchen table, where he placed the folder before sitting down. I was able to get a better look at the file while I poured us each a cup of coffee.

Agent Oliver opened the main folder and spread its contents out in front of him like a buffet. As I joined him at the table, I scanned the labels on the smorgasbord of files.

Each of the people we'd interviewed appeared to have a file on their own. In addition, some files were labeled with names I didn't recognize. Some stray sheets of paper left in the main folder seemed to be official reports and whatever other inner-bureau paperwork had been generated. I also saw what looked like financial statements bearing the Peterson Construction logo, and bank statements from a number of different local banks.

I handed Agent Oliver one of the two coffee mugs as I took a seat across from him. I wanted to ask the FBI man what he was doing here and how I was supposed to help but words failed me. At least words that didn't sound like I was still complaining. I really needed a massage and some relaxation time. I made a mental note to find a massage therapist in town and get that scheduled. I was sure it would change my outlook on life.

"This is the case file on Scott Curtis's homicide," Agent Oliver began. "I'm interested in your thoughts."

"I . . . uh . . . I don't think that's such a good idea." In fact, I thought that was a lousy idea. Even when the words of He Who Waits came rushing back to me.

"The spirits will not rest until justice is served. It is your *ozuye* to see justice done."

I must have looked slightly guilty or something because Agent Oliver's steel grey eyes bored into me until I started to turn away. Once again, I thought that if this was how he acted around co-workers, I didn't doubt that those he interrogated would easily crack under the weight of his gaze.

I sipped my coffee in an effort to clear my head. When I glanced back at Agent Oliver, the cold, hard edge had left his eyes and was replaced by something almost representing compassion.

"Look, someone up my chain of command thinks you can help," he began. His voice took on a tone that would have been defeatist in someone else. In him, it sounded almost reassuring and I wondered if it wasn't another interrogation technique—"Good Cop," now starring Special Agent Joseph Oliver—since the jerk routine obviously hadn't worked to his advantage. "I'll be honest. I'm not so sure you can help. But nothing indicates that you were directly involved. So, I'd like to hear your thoughts."

It was one of the few times in my life I found myself totally speechless. I couldn't even think of a smart-ass comment. Then again, I didn't take compliments well and I was pretty sure those seven words were as close to a compliment as Agent Oliver would ever speak.

Clearing my throat, I grabbed the closest file folder and began to leaf through the pages. I was positive this wasn't the complete file and some sentences had been crossed out with a dark magic marker.

"Mark and Heather Tomasello. Scott's neighbors," said Agent Oliver. "They both work nights, so they weren't home the night Scott was killed. Didn't really know him, other than to say hello in the halls."

Scanning the few pages in the file verified what Agent Oliver had said. I closed the folder and reached for another thin one.

Agent Oliver summarized it as I flipped through the pages.

"Patricia Griffin. Neighbor on the other side. She wasn't home that night either. She worked until six o'clock and then had dinner in downtown Rapid City before catching the seven o'clock movie at the Elks. She had actually talked to Scott a little, but didn't know him well. Occasionally, the two of them would end up at the apartment complex's workout room at the same time. Again, she said he was quiet, a bit shy, very private about his personal life, same thing we heard yesterday. There's no indication that the two were romantically involved, or even friendly beyond seeing each other in the halls or at the gym."

"He just had the two neighbors?" I asked.

This time Agent Oliver reached for a file. "No. There is a couple who live across the hall from our victim. Herb and Irma Taylor. They're elderly. In fact, the husband can't hear much of anything without his hearing aids and he refuses to wear them. They were home, but watching television with the sound turned way up."

"So they didn't hear anything, right?"

Agent Oliver smiled ruefully as he shook his head. "Not a sound."

"Great."

Agent Oliver shrugged and reached for another folder, this one thicker. The label on the tab stated KEVIN KIRK.

"That's the guy we talked to yesterday. The one from the root beer plant."

"Yep," replied Agent Oliver. "And I don't like him. He wasn't being totally honest with us."

I knew that since He Who Waits had told me, but I didn't know how Agent Oliver knew for certain. I also knew that even though Kevin may have been involved he didn't kill Scott—a woman did—so whatever Kevin was hiding probably didn't have anything to do with Scott's murder. How was I going to make Agent Oliver believe that without sounding like more of a crackpot the he already thought I was?

"Um . . . do you think Kevin did it?" I asked.

Agent Oliver took a drink of his coffee before answering. "Honestly? No, I don't. I think I told you that yesterday. But I do know he's hiding something and I want to find out what."

I took a chance by saying "It won't matter. Kevin Kirk didn't do it. He doesn't have the . . . fortitude. I mean, he has the skills and certainly the rage to commit murder, but this was well thought out, right? That's . . . um . . . that's not his strong suit."

Rather than admonishing me, Agent Oliver just nodded. "I think you might be right."

Two compliments in less than an hour? I was pretty sure that was some sort of personal record for Agent Oliver.

"Honestly, I feel the same about his girlfriend, Tina." In unfamiliar territory with Agent Oliver as it was, I decided it couldn't hurt to take the conversation a little further. "She's seems like a 'crime of passion' type and not someone who would plan out an actual murder."

The FBI agent only nodded his agreement.

We sat in silence for a few moments. Agent Oliver seemed to be staring into his coffee mug while I closed my eyes and rested my head on my hands, elbows on the table. I would have yelled at the kids for sitting slouched that way, but I really needed to concentrate. Something Kevin had said was bothering me and I was trying to replay the interview in my mind.

Finally, I got a grasp on that niggling memory trying to elude me. "I think I've got something," I said timidly.

I was unwilling to break the silence, not just because of what I had remembered, but also because of how it might sound. I still wasn't sure enough of myself, at least in this capacity, to make any bold, declarative statements. "Didn't Kevin say something about Scott arguing with someone? Some woman? What did you find out about that?"

Agent Oliver sighed. "Not much. We're checking over Scott's cell phone records to see if we can determine who he might have been talking to. It's been long enough that the number wasn't in his phone any longer, so we have to actually go through the service provider. I should have those records this afternoon."

"Dang. I thought that might have been the key." I hadn't realized I'd spoken aloud until Agent Oliver replied.

"It still might be. But if it is, experience tells me there's another trail to whoever she is."

That made sense to me, but I wasn't sure how to find this other trail. Neither He Who Waits nor Scott himself had told me who killed him, so the other trail didn't have any otherworldly signposts for me to read. At least not ones I hadn't already explored.

Agent Oliver collected the folders on the table, then set a few aside. "We know Scott was arguing with a woman. The only woman directly connected to him is his boss, Michaela Davis. She's the only female we can find who had consistent, close, personal contact with Scott."

I remembered Michaela, the head of the accounting department at Peterson Construction. I couldn't imagine her physically harming anyone. Her style seemed more subtle than that.

My face must have given me away, because Agent Oliver scrutinized me closely. "What is it?" he asked.

"Nothing really. I just don't think Michaela would have physically harmed Scott. He worked for her. And they were dating, I'm sure of it. If they'd broken up, she could have made his life miserable at work and I think that would have been enough for her— more than enough, probably." I paused before continuing. "In fact, I think she probably would prefer it that way. To make someone miserable right where she could see it and, I dunno, relish the thought of it. I think most women would. We can be a little vindictive that way."

"You really think they were dating?"

119

"I'm sure of it." I wasn't completely sure how to proceed with this line, but I was pretty sure Agent Oliver should know who Scott's girlfriend was. "The way Michaela talked about Scott, it was the way women talk about secret relationships. The tone of her voice, her facial expressions. And it would make sense why no one else knew who his mystery woman was. But I still don't think she killed him."

My companion remained silent.

"Besides, Michaela didn't sound like a spurned lover when we interviewed her. She said Scott was a good employee. She didn't say how rotten he was, which is what a jilted woman would have done."

Agent Oliver's eyebrows rose as he nodded in agreement. "I think you might be on to something there. But passions are an interesting thing. Who's to say Michaela didn't decide to kill him after a fight?"

The FBI agent pulled the file with Michaela's name on the tab out of the stack and set it aside. "I'll check her alibi again and run a background check on her. How sure are you that they were dating?"

I remembered the image I'd had of Michaela and Scott enjoying a nice dinner and movie. "Very," I replied. "But with that no-fraternization policy, it's no wonder they didn't socialize with other couples."

Agent Oliver nodded in agreement as he took another folder from the stack and handed it to me. This one bore the name of Mark Peterson, Michaela and Scott's boss.

"What do you want me to do with this?"

"Read it," ordered the FBI agent.

"He didn't kill Scott. A woman did. I know it."

Agent Oliver resorted back to the scowl I was so used to.

Looking through the sanitized file didn't impress me any more then meeting Mark Peterson in person. He still reminded me of a stereotypical used car salesman—a slimy and crooked man who would tell you anything to complete the sale.

"He's managed to stay just inside the law," said Agent Oliver, as I flipped through the pages. "He may not be doing anything illegal, but he's not completely moral either. Not that his father ran the business much better."

I reached across Agent Oliver and picked up the prospectus information wielding the Peterson Construction logo. Quickly skimming through the details, I didn't see anything out of the ordinary, but my college accounting class had been a long time ago.

"Nothing there raised a red flag for me," he said, indicating to the pages I was reviewing. "But accounting isn't my specialty. I sent a copy of that to our forensic accountant. She's working on it."

"Skimming over this, nothing jumps out at me, either." I flipped a few more pages. "Mind if I borrow it?"

"Be my guest." Agent Oliver began to gather the files we had spread across the table. "In fact, why don't you look through these, too?"

He handed me the other financial statements he'd brought. Personal information had been blacked out, so there were no account numbers or even individual names on the papers, but the deposits and withdraws from the various accounts were there.

I agreed to go through the figures, somewhat amazed at Agent Oliver's attitude change. I started to ask him about his sudden switch in demeanor when he stood up to leave.

"I'll call you later. Let me know if you find anything that might be helpful." He didn't say another word as he showed himself out of the house.

Were manners a thing of the past? Did no one ever say goodbye before leaving? Or was there something about me that attracted disappearing males?

At least I knew I would be able to count on my loving, scientific-minded husband to still be around when all this was said and done.

I hoped.

22

There was too much information floating around in my head, and none of it was stuff I really wanted there. Agent Oliver had let me see most the information pertaining to Scott Curtis's murder, but I still didn't know anything that would help him solve it. Especially since names and numbers had been blacked out. I wasn't sure if that information would help, but I had the distinct impression of trying to put together a jigsaw puzzle without all the pieces. Not for the first time, I was frustrated with He Who Waits for forcing me to call that tip line, and with my mother for convincing my father to try and "help" by having me assist with the case. There really should have been someone who cared more about mysteries. That would have made more sense.

"But you care about people, *Cuwitku*," came the grandfatherly voice of He Who Waits. "Caring about people is more than enough. It is the reason you were chosen."

"Yeah, well, I don't want to do this."

He Who Waits chuckled. "So you have said. And, yet, you are trying to find the killer. You are working hard to assist the *wawanyake*. You are spending time to find answers. You are not just giving the information and then washing your hands of it. You do this all because you care."

For once his words didn't seem so cryptic, they actually made sense to me. Either I was starting to accept my so-called *ozuye*, or I was finally ready for the loony bin after all.

As usual, I didn't need to vocalize the thought for He Who Waits to add his comments. "Your heart is starting to speak to your head. You are fulfilling your destiny. You are helping to find justice."

I didn't reply. There was nothing to say. Plus, the phone rang, ensuring I didn't have to answer the shaman.

I was surprised at the voice on the other end of the line. A woman asked for Ms. Baker. Something about her terse tone rubbed me the wrong way almost immediately. It took me a moment to place it, and even then I wasn't sure it was the secretary from Peterson Construction. I couldn't imagine anyone else with that accent, though.

"This is Mrs. Baker. Is this Elke?"

"*Ja.* Um, yes." She sounded almost relieved that I had

recognized her. "I must speak with you."

Except for the fact her voice annoyed me; I didn't get any major internal warning bells going off, although it probably wouldn't have changed anything if I had. "Sure, what's up?"

"No, I mean, in person. Face-to-face," Elke said. "I need to speak with you about . . . well, it's about Scott's murder." Her voice had gotten much softer, as if trying hard not to be overheard. "I think I have some information you might need."

I could feel the grin spread over my face. This might soon be over and I could get back to my normal life. I couldn't keep the elation out of my voice. "Really? Great! I'll call Agent—"

"No! I mean, I don't know how important this really is. I'd prefer to tell just you. Privately, I mean."

"Oh, well, I suppose." I tried explaining that this wasn't my area of expertise, but I couldn't remember exactly how Agent Oliver had introduced me when we interviewed people at Peterson Construction, so I didn't want to protest too much. Besides, this might be the break the agent needed to catch Scott's killer. With my newfound confidence, I couldn't just let that opportunity slide.

Elke and I agreed on a meeting place in downtown Rapid City. I told her I would be there in twenty minutes.

There were still no neon lights flashing danger in my mind, or Shamanic words telling me to stay away, so I went. But not before leaving a note for Matt in case he made it home before I got back. I didn't want him to worry. I also called the mother of the teenage girls across the street to see if she would watch Zack, Maddie, and Kenzie if I didn't make it home before the bus got there. We had already implemented a "safe word system" so our kids would know it was okay and the girl's mother knew the word. I had no doubt that my three would enjoy some time with the teens.

It took me a few minutes to find my keys, and even longer to find my cell phone. I really should find a place to store these things, I thought, mentally adding that to my to-do-list for this afternoon. Sometimes making a new house feel like home is even harder then physically moving.

If only there had been a sign of the danger to come.

23

By the time I arrived at the coffee shop we'd agreed on, I was only three minutes late.

As I started to get out of the car, I heard a tap on the passenger's window. Startled, I looked over to see Elke motioning for me to roll the window down.

My vehicle had power windows, but I hit the wrong button. Instead of rolling down the window, I unlocked the doors. Elke must have thought that's what I meant to do because she opened the passenger door and climbed right in.

"This place is too crowded," she said. "What I want to tell you is too personal, too private. Can we go somewhere else?"

Being so new to the area I didn't know where else to go.

"Can't you just tell me here? I mean, my car is pretty private even if we are in a public parking lot." I tried to make a joke of it.

Elke reached into her hobo-style purse and pulled out a pistol. "Not private enough."

My heart started beating so fast I thought it might explode and my mouth went completely dry. It occurred to me that it was a good thing I'd gone to the bathroom before I left the house or I'd probably be peeing my pants right about now. It was an irrational thought, to be sure, but I chalked it up to stress and never having had a gun pointed at me before.

"Let's go." Elke waved the gun and I didn't see as I had much choice.

We reached Omaha Street and headed east toward the airport. She didn't talk much as I drove, just to give directions, but she kept her hand on the pistol in her lap, pointed right at me.

In my nervousness, I could have sworn my heart was beating so loudly Elke could hear it. My palms were sweating so profusely that I kept rubbing them on my pant legs in a futile attempt to dry them.

At one point, I tried wiping the sweat from my hand and glancing at Elke at the same time. I swerved a little into oncoming traffic, causing the other driver to honk his horn and flip me the bird.

"Don't try anything stupid," Elke ordered. "Don't make me hurt you."

That killed any plans I may have had for an active escape. And, of course, I couldn't find a cop car, so any thoughts of reckless driving to get pulled over weren't panning out either. Why was there was never a cop around when you needed one?

By the time we'd past the turnoff for the airport, I could stand the silence no longer. Businesses didn't exist in this area and the houses were getting farther and farther apart. Even the ranches were becoming fewer. If I remembered correctly, the road ended up in the Badlands and I was pretty sure things would get ugly for me if we made it that far. Fear was starting to be replaced with resignation and I wondered if that was one of the stages of grief.

At that moment, my cell phone rang. This could be my chance. It had to be Matt. Who else would call me? How could I get a message to him without Elke killing me?

Panicked, I looked at the woman in my passenger seat. "Answer it," she said, raising the gun to my chest. "But don't be stupid."

I swallowed hard before answering the call. "Hello?"

"Hey, Cerri, it's me, Wendy." Wendy's voice seemed unnaturally loud and cheerful, but I wasn't sure if it was my extreme stress or not. I hoped Elke couldn't hear her, but I was too terrified to take any chances. Where was He Who Waits and all his wisdom when I had a gun pointed at me?

"Wendy, this really isn't a good time." I glanced at Elke. "Can I call you back?"

"I just need to tell you this one thing," my sister began. I couldn't get a word in edgewise as she told me about the costume she'd just sold on the internet. Wendy sewed period costumes as a hobby and had recently decided to try and earn a little extra cash selling them.

My sister, who never wanted to talk on the phone, picked the moment I had a gun pointed at me to call. The Universe had a strange sense of humor.

When I finally got a word in edgewise, I decided to take my chance. Before speaking, I glanced at Elke who was looking more annoyed as the seconds ticked by.

"Hey, Wen, it really isn't a good time. I have to go. Give Molly a big hug and kiss for me." I flipped the phone shut before Wendy could ask me anything else. I prayed that she would think my wanting Wendy to kiss her diseased and grotesque pet was an odd request. Hopefully odd enough to get word to Matt or Agent Oliver and I'd be saved from the psycho woman sitting next to me.

Sadly, it was the best plan I could come up with at the time.

After a few more minutes, Elke told me to turn right. We were no longer on a paved road, but a well-used gravel one instead. A few turns later, Elke had me stop the car and turn off the engine.

I tried to take in our surroundings. We seemed to be at an outdoor shooting range right at the edge of the Badlands. No one else was around since the temperature was in the lower forties. Combined with thirty mile an hour winds, it made it much too cold for anyone but the most avid of shooters. And since this wasn't a weekend, the place was deserted.

There would be no one to save me.

I wasn't ready to give up just yet, though. Without seeing an escape route, I decided to try another tactic—delay.

"You did it, didn't you? You killed Scott." My voice cracked and I felt a burning sensation at the back of my throat. I didn't want to lose my composure, but I honestly wasn't sure it would matter much anyway. The end result was bound to be the same.

Even though I was expecting it, Elke's matter-of-fact response threw me for a loop. "Yes. I did." Her voice held little emotion and I wondered briefly at how cold and callus she must be to have so little feeling attached to taking someone's life.

"Why?"

"It needed to be done." Elke looked at me as if I were a little child who didn't understand the simplest of instructions. "Get out of the car."

I didn't think it wise to argue, so I stepped out of the vehicle. I had the foresight to grab the keys, hoping I'd be able to make a break for it later. Elke snatched them from my hands as she exited the car. Even as she walked around to my side of the vehicle, Elke kept the gun leveled at my chest.

None of my plans were going the way I wanted. I made a mental note to enroll in self-defense classes if I made it out of this alive. Or purchase a container of pepper spray to keep on my key chain. Or both.

"But, why? Why kill him? What did he do to you?"

Elke didn't answer for what seemed like an eternity. As I watched, Elke took a lighter and a pack of cigarettes from her pocket, pulled one out and lit it. When she finally spoke, she sounded almost shocked. "Do you really not know?"

When I refused to answer, Elke continued. "Scott was an accountant. He handled the money that came into the company."

I nodded and remained silent, hoping to keep Elke talking. For awhile, it seemed to work.

"Scott and Tom were friends. They were always together and Scott was smart. He had this memory on him. Scott could remember numbers like no one else you've ever seen." Elke's eyes got a far-away look as she started to reminisce.

I wondered if I could make it back inside my vehicle before she noticed. I took a step to the right, breaking Elke's trance.

"I don't know why I'm bothering to tell you any of this." Elke shook her head before continuing, her voice harsher now. "Anyway, Scott was getting Tom to tell him some of the numbers being billed. Because of Scott's damn memory, he knew the numbers weren't adding up."

"I'm not sure why that meant you had to kill him." It occurred to me that if I participated more in the conversation, maybe I could move around a little without her noticing. "Just because he knew the numbers were different? Wouldn't the boss want to know if someone was stealing?"

Elke's laugh reminded me again of nails on a chalkboard. "You are really dense, aren't you?" She rolled her eyes, but continued with her story. "Mr. Peterson already knew. Who do you think was taking the money?"

I looked at her in amazement as I took a step backward. "You mean the owner was skimming off the top? And you think that's okay?"

Pure hatred flashed in Elke's eyes. "Yes, that's okay. Why wouldn't it be?" When I didn't respond, she continued. "Mr. Peterson is amazing. He inherited the company from his father. Back then Peterson Construction was barely getting by. Now we have contracts all over the country. That type of growth doesn't just happen. Mr. Peterson had to make some . . . unusual business dealings in the past and had gotten in over his head. It's his company. He should be able to spend the money however he would like. It's not like Mr. Peterson isn't a generous man, you know."

Elke's voice had changed. No longer was it as cold as steel, some warmth had wormed its way in as she discussed her boss. Even her features had softened as she spoke of him.

"You love him, don't you?" I asked, taking another step closer to the car. "You had to protect him."

She made a guttural noise that sounded like a cross between a snort and a chuckle. "I guess you aren't as stupid as I thought. Yes, I love Mark Peterson. I would do anything for him. It's hard enough having to share him with his wife. Some junior accountant with a conscious certainly wasn't going to take him away from me."

The whole thing was starting to make sense to me. I took yet another step closer to my Jeep. "So Scott was going to turn your boss in to the Internal Revenue Service or something? And you didn't want Mr. Peterson to get in any trouble, right?"

"He could have gone to jail! Of course I was going to protect him!"

The next step I took must have been a little too big because Elke again waved the gun at me, motioning for me to move back. As I did, I watched her face, which had again taken a crazed look. I sent up a silent prayer that someone would show up.

Soon.

I needed to calm Elke again, but didn't want to risk taking another step yet. "So you got rid of Scott before he could turn Peterson in?"

"Michaela would never have noticed the discrepancies on her own. She's too stupid. She only got the job because her father was friends with Mr. Peterson." Jealousy had started to creep into Elke's voice and it wasn't a pretty sound. "I've seen all the accounts and Mr. Peterson had done a great job of moving the money around. Without Scott's memory, no one would have noticed. And then Scott started digging up more information. He was close to finding out what was going on."

"So he had to be stopped," I reiterated, "in order to protect Mark Peterson."

Elke nodded smugly. "Exactly."

"Couldn't you just try to get him fired?" There had to be some other recourse besides murder.

She snorted. "It wasn't as if I didn't try. I knew about Mike and him, but every time I tried to tell Mark he changed the subject. The more I thought about it, the more I decided Michaela might be the one fired and I couldn't have that, either."

"I see." Clearly keeping Elke talking wasn't presenting me with vast opportunities for escape.

Where was He Who Waits when I needed him?

24

I didn't know what to do. This was not a situation I'd ever found myself in before and frankly I had never contemplated being in. I mean, who plans to have a crazy woman shoot them? No one I knew.

I said a silent prayer hoping that some deity somewhere would hear it. Deep down, I wasn't sure.

As I was about to give up, He Who Waits appeared behind Elke. "Keep her talking, *Cuwitku*. Do not give up."

There was nothing more for me to say to Elke. She'd told me why she killed Scott and, clearly, she was intent on killing me to keep her secret.

"Do you know I have children?" My voice cracked with emotion as it hit me that I may never see them or Matt again.

"Well, that sucks for you, doesn't it?" Elke's voice held no compassion, but the sarcasm dripping from it shocked me. She waved the gun again and for a moment it occurred to me that at least I was standing downrange from her if she decided to shoot. It wasn't a logical thought, but nothing in this situation struck me as logical.

"Cough, *Cuwitku*! Make a loud noise!" He Who Waits yelled so loudly I thought Elke must have heard him.

It took a moment for me to understand what the shaman was saying, but when I did, I coughed. To Elke it must have sounded like I was having a tuberculosis attack or something. Confused, I didn't know why He Who Waits wanted me to make noise, but I didn't have a reason to doubt him.

Faking my coughing fit, I buckled over, covering my face with both hands, my mind working furiously for an escape plan.

That's when I heard them. I looked up to see cars driving up the gravel road toward the shooting range where Elke and I were. I could begin to see the dust rising up from the other side of the hill.

The cavalry has arrived, I thought, relief sweeping over me.

He Who Waits must have been eavesdropping on my thoughts again, because he shot me a look that said he didn't appreciate the reference.

In the nanosecond it took for me to offer a silent apology for offending the shaman, Elke crossed the distance between us. I thought again how useful pepper spray would be in this situation. The gun in her hand remained pointed at me.

Before I could react, Elke had maneuvered herself behind me grabbing my right arm and twisting it painfully.

"Shut up! I will kill you," Elke hissed into my ear.

25

The cars pulled into the parking lot of the shooting range. Two white SUVs with Pennington County's gold five-pointed star led the pack, every light on the vehicle flashing. Behind them, I recognized Agent Oliver's non-descript sedan. His car also had a flashing red light on the dashboard that gave no doubt the driver was conducting official law enforcement business.

I'd never been so happy to see anyone.

I could barely take in the scene through the settling dust when men stepped out of each vehicle, guns drawn.

"Let her go," one of the deputies shouted.

It didn't work any better here than it did in the movies. Elke refused to release me and I was sure her trigger finger had started twitching.

I heard her gasp in my ear and felt her turn my body to one side. "*Mein Gott*," she whispered. "My God. Is that him? Scott? Why is he here? How is it possible?"

She was right. Scott was there. He had materialized off to one side of the group and He Who Waits was standing on the other side of the apparition.

Fascinated with the sight before her, Elke started mumbling in German. Not being fluent in the language, I didn't understand much of what she said.

Elke pulled me back a little, which was pretty much her downfall. Literally.

As she yanked me, I scrambled to keep up. Unfortunately, there was a gopher hole which I managed to find.

No, I'm still not entirely sure how that happened or if I could have made it happen that way if I had tried.

Somehow in the midst tripping, my foot ended up behind her and she consequently tripped over me. Elke landed on her backside, I landed on top of her, wrenching my injured leg.

Elke grabbed me, trying to keep me where I was. Thankfully, she dropped the gun as she fell, so I didn't need to worry about that anymore.

I jabbed her in the ribs. Hard. I was trying to push her away from me and get up at the same time, my foot still firmly planted in the hole.

Only seconds later I was being pulled off her and Elke was being handcuffed.

I heard Agent Oliver recite the Miranda rights as a paramedic led me to an ambulance.

The shooting range was devoid of otherworldly entities until I found myself sitting alone in the passenger's seat of Agent Oliver's car of about thirty minutes later. I'd been given a clean bill of health, but my nerves were still shot.

"You have done well, *Cuwitku*. Justice has been found for Scott Curtis."

"I tried." I closed my eyes and leaned against the seat. More than anything I wanted to get home to my family.

"You did well. He wishes to thank you."

I opened my eyes to see He Who Waits and Scott standing only a few feet away. No one else seemed to notice the apparitions.

Since I'd never been good with compliments or displays of gratitude, I muttered, "Tell him not to mention it. Seriously, don't mention it."

A faint chuckle resonated as my visitors vanished.

26

A few days later Agent Oliver again graced my doorstep with his presence.

I started in before he had a chance to speak. "Thank you. Thank you for saving my life."

He just nodded. "I came out here to thank you, actually."

"Thank me?" I invited him into the house, and we sat in the living room. The scene reminded me of the first time the FBI agent had darkened my door. This time, however, I was much less nervous and he was much less of a jerk.

"Yep. You, and . . . whoever you get your information from, were able to help us more then you realize."

Afraid to ask questions, I sat staring at him.

"It would have taken us longer to put the pieces together if you hadn't stumbled on the relationship between Michaela Davis and Scott Curtis. Then when the forensic accountant found some discrepancies in the Peterson Construction financials, it focused the investigation on someone there."

I had guessed most of this, but it was nice to be able to have my suspicions confirmed.

Agent Oliver continued. "Then when Matt got the call from your sister that something was wrong, we were able to triangulate your cell phone signal. Good thing you didn't shut it off."

I shrugged. I didn't want to admit that I hadn't thought of making sure the phone stayed on so someone could find me. I was more grateful Elke hadn't thought to make me shut it off.

Agent Oliver spent the next few minutes recapping the arrest from his point of view. It didn't matter to me. I knew what had taken place.

"So what will happen to her? To Elke Thompson?"

"There will be a trial and you'll have to testify for the government. I have no doubt she'll be convicted of Scott Curtis's murder and the attempted murder of you."

"Any idea why she picked Devils Tower?"

Agent Oliver shook his head. "No. Other then she thought it was secluded enough to not get caught and since it's in Wyoming, there was very little to tie her directly to the crime scene. The Tower is fairly secluded. There aren't any towns of more then a few thousand people there. And it was a location that had nothing to do directly with her or with Peterson Construction."

"So the Tower, itself, wasn't significant to her?"

"We don't think so. She isn't saying much, but the theory is that it was close enough to be convenient, yet far enough away to divert suspicion from her and Mark Peterson and the rest of the construction company. I think if Elke had known about the dart league and Kevin Kirk, she may have murdered Scott in a way that would have placed more doubt in that direction."

I let his hypothesis soak in for a few moments.

Agent Oliver stood to leave and I followed him to the door. Before walking out, he turned and extended his hand to me. Tentatively, I shook it.

"I'm sorry about accusing you," he said. "No hard feelings."

"No, no hard feelings," I repeated. "You were doing your job."

He looked as if he would like to say something else.

"What?"

"I know your father is a consultant with the CIA," he began. "That's how we were forced to work together."

I rolled my eyes, realizing I had yet to inform Mother how much I resented her meddling.

"It's okay," Agent Oliver continued. "You really were a big help on this one. I'd like to keep your information if I run across any other cases I think you could . . . consult on."

Eyeing him suspiciously, I asked, "Does this mean you believe I got the information in a dream?"

He shrugged. "Maybe not a dream, but I did see you not fall that day downtown. Something's helping you out."

With that he left. Good timing, too, because my phone rang. It was Mother.

"What can I do for you, Ma?"

"So you have survived your adventure?" came the response on the other end of the line. "Tell me all about it."

I recapped my experience and what I had learned from Agent Oliver, Mother remained silent the entire time. When I was finished, she started to chuckle.

"What is so funny? It was actually pretty frightening."

"I know, lass," Mother said. "I was just thinking about your sister's movies. She told you about the movies in the hall, correct?"

"Yeah, some Spielberg DVDs, right?" As Mother continued to laugh, the significance of the movie titles finally hit me. "I get it. *Close Encounters of the Third Kind* because the murder was at Devils Tower."

Mother agreed.

"And *Twilight Zone* because this was a pretty freaky experience for me, right?"

Again, Mother agreed.

"But why *E.T.*?" I paused. "Oh, wait! Elke Thompson. ET. Someone was trying to tell me she was the murderer."

"Now you have it." I could hear the joy in Mother's voice, as if I had produced something she'd long been awaiting. It felt good to make her proud of me.

"And now that it's over I can go back to my normal life," I announced.

Mother's last words before hanging up drained my feeling of euphoria. "If that's what you think, dear."

Acknowledgements

I would like to thank my editor Deb Ledford and everyone else at Indigo Sea Press. Thank you to retired Douglas County (Nebraska) Deputy Sheriff Jim Westcott who helped with some of the law enforcement aspects of the novel. A special thank you to my mom and dad, who let me bounce many ideas off them; my husband and daughters, who helped with the story plot; members of the Black Hills Writers Group for their thoughts and critiques; and numerous friends who didn't look at me strangely when I asked some off-the-wall questions.